Truffles a Cove Cozy Mystery Series Book 6

By Leena Clover

Copyright © Leena Clover, Author 2019

All rights reserved. No part of this publication may be reproduced, stored in a retrieval system, or transmitted, in any form, or by any means (electronic, mechanical, photocopying, recording or otherwise) without the prior written permission of the author.

This book is a work of fiction. Names, characters, places, organizations and incidents are either products of the author's imagination or used fictitiously. Any resemblance to actual events, places, organizations or persons, living or dead, is entirely coincidental.

First Published – January 27, 2019

CHAPTER 1	5
CHAPTER 2	17
CHAPTER 3	30
CHAPTER 4	42
CHAPTER 5	55
CHAPTER 6	68
CHAPTER 7	80
CHAPTER 8	92
CHAPTER 9	103
CHAPTER 10	115
CHAPTER 11	127
CHAPTER 12	139
CHAPTER 13	152
CHAPTER 14	165

CHAPTER 15	177
CHAPTER 16	189
CHAPTER 17	201
CHAPTER 18	213
CHAPTER 19	225
CHAPTER 20	238
EPILOGUE	250
ACKNOWLEDGEMENTS	253
JOIN MY NEWSLETTER	256

Chapter 1

It was a scorching summer day in Pelican Cove. At the Boardwalk Café, Jenny King hummed a tune as she gently poured scalded cream into a bowl of chopped chocolate. She was trying her hand at making truffles. Jenny and her friends had a big sweet tooth and they all loved chocolate. She couldn't wait to see their reaction when she placed a platter of her fancy truffles before them.

Jenny added orange zest to the chocolate mixture and spooned in some orange liquer. The mixture was poured into fancy moulds. Jenny hurried to place the trays in the refrigerator as she heard a flurry of footsteps.

Two young women burst into the kitchen, vying for Jenny's attention.

"Something smells good," Heather Morse said, closing her eyes as she took a deep breath. "What's cooking, Jenny?"

Heather was a bold, attractive 35 year old woman who believed in making her own rules. She called herself Jenny's wing woman.

"Are you making your six layer chocolate cake?" Molly

asked.

Tall and scrawny with thick Coke bottle glasses, she was the same age as Heather. The two couldn't have been more different.

"It's a surprise," Jenny admitted. "It's a new recipe. You will be my first tasters, promise."

"That's not fair!" Heather grumbled. "Can't you give us a hint?"

The friends parried back and forth, laughing and teasing each other.

Jenny felt a warm glow in her heart as she gazed lovingly at her friends. She couldn't imagine life without them.

Dumped and discarded by her cheating husband of twenty years, Jenny had sought shelter in the small town of Pelican Cove. Jenny had been at a crossroads when her aunt Star opened her home and her heart to her. She grabbed her aunt's invitation like a lifeline, arriving at the small barrier island off the coast of Virginia without any expectations. She had never imagined the path her life would take.

Jenny started working at the local café at her aunt's insistence. Her skills in the kitchen had earned instant approval with locals and tourists alike. The Boardwalk

Café soared in popularity and Jenny flourished along with it. People flocked from far and wide to eat her tasty food.

Jenny had bought a seaside mansion with her divorce settlement and proudly called Pelican Cove home. She had found purpose in life. She made lifelong friends and then she had found love.

"Are you dreaming about Adam?" Heather trilled in her ear.

Adam Hopkins was the sheriff of Pelican Cove. He was also Jenny's betrothed. The two had finally set the date for their wedding after a long engagement. Jenny's friends were very excited about the impending nuptials and were urging her to start planning for the big day.

"We had lunch together," Jenny admitted with a blush.

"That doesn't answer my question," Heather said with a laugh. "The big day isn't far away, Jenny. It's high time we started planning for it."

"Save the wedding planning for another day," Molly interrupted, glancing at the clock on the kitchen wall. "We need to get going."

"She's right," Jenny said. "I don't want to miss a minute of the town meeting. All the funny stuff seems to happen at the beginning."

"Are you saying the town hall meeting is a joke?" Heather asked in mock horror.

The three friends laughed out loud.

"Where's Betty Sue?" Jenny asked, referring to Heather's grandmother.

Betty Sue was a formidable woman in her eighties, and wielded a lot of power in the small town. She was the direct descendant of James Morse, the founder of Pelican Cove. James Morse had travelled south from New England with his family in 1837. He had bought the island for $125 and named it Morse Isle. He built a house for his family on a large tract of land. Fishing provided him with a livelihood, so did floating wrecks. He sent for a friend or two from up north. They came and settled on the island with their families. They in turn invited their friends. Morse Isle soon became a thriving community.

Being a barrier island, it took a battering in the great storm of 1962. Half the island was submerged forever. Most of that land had belonged to the Morse family. A new town emerged in the aftermath of the storm and it was named Pelican Cove.

Betty Sue had retained the Morse name even after marriage. Heather was the last Morse on the island, and the Morse bloodline was in danger of extinction unless she got married and produced a young one soon.

"Grandma's already there," Heather told Jenny. "There's going to be a big announcement."

"Must be something about the fall festival," Molly said. "It's going to be bigger and better than anything we ever put on."

"Didn't sound like it," Heather said with a frown.

"Why are we standing here playing the guessing game?" Jenny asked, pulling off her apron. "Let's head over there. We'll find out soon enough."

Pelican Cove was experiencing a bright and sunny summer day. Sun worshippers lined the beach, sprawled on colorful beach towels and chairs, working on their tan. Kids laughed as they frolicked in the water, the little ones squealing in delight as they jumped over the ocean waves. The sun had moved closer to the horizon but the days were long with sunset several hours away.

The girls walked along the boardwalk, arm in arm, chattering nineteen to a dozen. Soon they were inside the town hall building, greeting friends and acquaintances.

"Jenny," a tall, older woman bellowed from the front. "I saved your seats."

The girls walked up to Star, Jenny's aunt. Star was an artist who painted seascapes of the surrounding region. Her art was popular among the tourists. Jenny had recently helped her set up a web portal for selling her work. Star could barely keep up with the demand.

Like Jenny, Star was a chicken necker. It was a term the islanders used for someone who wasn't born in the region. Star had been hitchhiking around the country in the seventies. She had arrived in Pelican Cove, fallen in love with the town and a local and never left.

"Where's my grandma?" Heather asked Star.

Star pointed toward a small stage at the front of the room. A few chairs were arranged behind the podium. Betty Sue sat in one of them.

"There's something big going on," Star told them. "That's why she's up there."

Nothing important happened in Pelican Cove without Betty Sue's approval. A short, plump woman stood at the podium and called for silence. The crowd gradually settled down.

Jenny noticed a couple of new faces and wondered who they were.

"Welcome!" The woman at the podium beamed at everyone. "I see we have a good turnout today. You won't be disappointed. We have a big announcement."

A tall, black haired man sprang up from the row behind Jenny.

"Wait a minute. I got something to say."

"We can talk about it later." The woman stared the man down.

Her name was Barb Norton and she was generally found at the helm of some committee or the other.

"No!" the man said flatly. "This is urgent. It affects the whole town."

People began to murmur and guess what the man was going to say.

Betty Sue Morse leaned forward and tapped the woman at the podium on the shoulder. Barb let out a big sigh.

"Very well, Peter Wilson," she said to the man. "But make it quick."

Peter Wilson whirled around and pointed to a young man slouching on a bench in the last row.

"You there," he roared. "Come forward. I want everyone in this room to see you properly."

The man stood up and blinked. He was one of the strangers Jenny had spotted earlier. She guessed he was in his early twenties, maybe a couple of years older than her son Nick. His blond hair stood up in tufts and his green eyes lit up as he smiled at the crowd. He ambled to the front of the room and stood there, his hands in his pockets.

"Who is this?" Barb Norton asked.

"I'm Tyler Jones," the boy smiled.

"Forget about his name," Peter Wilson dismissed. "He's a bloody nuisance, that's what he is."

"Mind your language!" Barb said sharply.

She looked at the boy called Tyler and gave him a motherly smile.

"What have you done?"

The boy shrugged and said nothing. Jenny noticed he was what the kids called 'cool'. He didn't appear to be ruffled at all.

"This young buck has made my life hell," Peter Wilson yelled, jabbing a finger at Tyler. "He stands in front of my house, playing his guitar and raising a ruckus. We need to drive him out of town."

"You play your guitar on the street?" Barb Norton

asked the young man.

Tyler nodded.

"I'm the troubadour. I filed my paperwork two months ago."

"Oh!" Barb's face relaxed and her shoulders settled. "Don't you play on the boardwalk?"

"Sometimes," Tyler said with a shrug. "I prefer the town square. I have a favorite spot near the gazebo."

"Right in front of my house, he means," Peter Wilson broke in. "Tell him to get out of town, Barb."

"No can do, Peter," Barb said. "He's the troubadour."

"What crap is that?"

"You're not from here, are you?" Barb said condescendingly. "The troubadours are a long standing tradition in Pelican Cove." She turned toward Betty Sue. "Isn't that right?"

Betty Sue bobbed her head. "My ancestor James Morse welcomed the first troubadour to the island back in 1892."

People began whispering among themselves and another murmur rose through the crowd. Jenny was as clueless as Peter Wilson. Heather brought her up to speed.

"Troubadours are traveling musicians. They write their own songs and compose their own music. It's been a while since one of them came along though. Not since I was in high school."

Peter Wilson heard her.

"Why does he sing on the street though?"

"It's my job," Tyler Jones said, rubbing a reddish mark on his cheek.

It looked like a birthmark of sorts.

"I sing and entertain people," Tyler continued.

"Who asked you to?" Peter Wilson fumed. "And why don't you sing in a pub or something?"

"Stop hounding the boy, Peter," Barb commanded from the podium. "There is a system in place here. As long as he filed his papers, he's good to go."

"So he's going to bang that guitar of his all hours of the day or night and there's nothing I can do?" Peter Wilson thundered. "What kind of joint are you running here?"

"The troubadours are known for their special brand of

music," Betty Sue spoke up. "Their music uplifts the soul."

"He's doing us a favor," Barb nodded.

"Sounds fishy to me," Peter Wilson grimaced. "I bet he's charging an arm and a leg for all that noise he makes."

Tyler Jones smiled. His whole face lit up and his eyes crinkled.

"I don't sing for money."

Peter Wilson's mouth dropped open.

"You don't say. Why do you stand in the sun all day making that awful racket?"

"That's enough, Peter," Barb Norton called out. "We need to move on to the next item."

Tyler Jones flashed another smile at the crowd and walked to the back of the room. Jenny decided to catch up with him after the meeting. She wondered if she could request him to pick a spot outside the Boardwalk Café. Her guests would surely enjoy some live music along with their food.

Barb Norton banged a gavel, trying to get the crowd's attention again.

"And now for an important announcement …"

"Wait!" a voice drawled from the back.

Jenny whirled around to see Tyler Jones raising his hand.

"What is it now, young man?" Barb asked.

"May I have a minute, please?" Tyler asked, standing up. "I need to file a grievance."

Chapter 2

The room erupted in chaos as everyone started speaking at the top of their voices. Barb Norton looked a bit flustered.

"You are not a resident of this town," she said. "I am not sure if you can address the town meeting with a complaint."

She turned around and gave Betty Sue a questioning look. There was a hurried conference between the two.

"I bet Grandma's loving all the attention," Heather said to Jenny.

"I may not be born here but I have lived in town for forty some years," Star said. "No outsider has ever been allowed to air a complaint at the town meeting."

"Does he have a problem with the town?" Molly wondered out loud.

Barb Norton and Betty Sue had come to a decision. Barb pounded her gavel again and waited for the noise to die down.

"This is highly irregular," Barb said. "But we have decided to hear you out. Why don't you come forward and state your problem?"

Tyler Jones smiled and ambled toward the front.

"Thank you," he began. "I want to report a trespasser. I filed my papers with the town in July and became the official troubadour of this town. According to the troubadour code, there can be only one of us in a town this size."

"That sounds right," Barb nodded. "What's the problem?"

Tyler pointed toward the back of the room.

"Him!"

A tall, middle aged man with a heavy beard stood up and bowed before the crowd, folding his hands together in greeting.

"He turned up last week," Tyler said. "He shouldn't be here at all."

"Can you please come forward, Sir?" Barb asked. "Please introduce yourself."

The man shuffled to the front of the room and stared at his feet. He mumbled in a low voice.

"Can you speak up?" Barb spoke loudly. "I can barely hear you. I'm sure the people at the back want to know your name."

"Ocean," the man said, clearing his throat. "My name is Ocean. I'm the troubadour."

"You may be *a* troubadour," Tyler Jones protested, "but you can't play your music in this town."

Ocean gave him a beatific smile.

"There's plenty of space for the both of us."

"I didn't make the rules," Tyler said, beginning to turn red. "You need to go somewhere else."

Peter Wilson was staring at the troubadours with an expression of disbelief.

"Here's a thought," he said, taking an aggressive stance. "Why don't you both pack your stuff and get the hell outta this town?"

The crowd guffawed. Barb Norton pounded her gavel again.

"This is not funny. The town has never faced this situation before."

"My permit is valid for six months," Tyler reminded Barb. "This is my turf until the end of the year."

"Why don't we discuss this later?" Barb reasoned. "We

are already running late."

"There is nothing to discuss," Ocean said. "We can both pick a spot in town."

"Don't you get it, man?" Tyler said, beginning to look provoked. "I got here first."

Jenny thought Tyler sounded childish.

"Let's have a sing-off," she suggested, springing up.

"What's that?" someone in the crowd asked.

"We'll have them play their music until one of them gives up," Jenny explained.

"Or they can each play five songs and we will vote on who's the best," Heather said, joining Jenny enthusiastically.

"You can't do that!" Tyler exclaimed. "What about my license? It gives me exclusive rights."

"Let's be reasonable, young man," Barb called out from her perch. "Don't forget the town gave you that permit. The town can revoke it anytime."

Tyler stomped a foot and pointed at the bearded man.

"Are you happy now, you gatecrasher?"

"All I want to do is entertain people with my music," Ocean said quietly.

His face had the same serene expression it had worn before. A smile tugged at the corner of his mouth.

"There's enough for the both of us," he added.

He held up his hand in a peace sign.

"I'm gonna wipe that irritating smile off your face," Tyler thundered.

He stalked out of the room without a backward glance. Ocean gave Barb a deep bow and turned to face the crowd. He bowed again and walked to the back of the room.

"I say we drive both these nut jobs out of town," Peter Wilson yelled.

Barb Norton banged the gavel again. A stream of sweat trickled down her forehead and beads of perspiration lined her upper lip. She dabbed at her face with a lace handkerchief. She cleared her throat and began. "We have an important item on the agenda today."

"Is it the fall festival?" someone cried from the crowd.

Barb held up a hand to ward off the fresh wave of

hecklers.

"This is a historic moment for Pelican Cove," Barb said, puffing up. "Mayor Franklin is stepping down."

Jenny knew the mayor of Pelican Cove was just a figurehead. Younger than Betty Sue, he was still pushing eighty. His bow tie was crooked and his suit was wrinkled. He sat on the podium next to Betty Sue, dozing with his neck lolling on his chest. Other than special appearances at town meetings, people barely saw him these days. Most of the civic work was done by his staff and a bunch of volunteers like Barb Norton.

Mayor Franklin sat up with a start when Betty Sue gave him a sharp nudge. He flashed a toothless smile and waved at the crowd.

The crowd had exploded in frenzy again.

Barb pounded the gavel with all her might and kept talking.

"Pelican Cove will have a mayoral election for the first time in fifty years. Nominations will be accepted at the town hall for the next three days."

"We know who's going to be first in line," Star said with a snort.

"Maybe I should throw my hat in," Heather joked. "I'm a Morse, after all."

"You can't be serious," Jenny said.

Barb concluded the meeting. Heather walked over to give Betty Sue a hand as she joined Jenny and the girls.

"We are coming to your place," Molly reminded Jenny. "What's for dinner?"

"Let's just grab a pizza," Heather suggested and everyone agreed.

The women started walking toward Mama Rosa's, the only pizza place in town.

"Did you know about the election?" Star asked Betty Sue. "You sure kept it close to your bosom."

"I knew about it," Betty Sue admitted. "But I was sworn to secrecy. Barb wanted to make a big splash. You know how she loves attention."

"Are you going to be our new mayor, Betty Sue?" Molly asked.

Betty Sue looked pensive as she shook her head.

"Ten years ago, I might have considered it. But I'm getting on now. The town doesn't need another Mayor

Franklin."

"She's right," Star said. "We need some young blood to steer us into the twenty first century."

"The twenty first century arrived two decades ago," Heather said with a smirk.

"Not in Pelican Cove," Star shot back.

"Give it a rest, you two," Jenny said, trying to diffuse the situation. "What toppings do you want on your pizza?"

Everyone wanted something different. They decided to go for one loaded veggie pizza and one loaded meat one.

A small crowd had gathered outside Mama Rosa's.

"Looks like everyone wants pizza for dinner," Heather joked.

"I don't think that's it," Molly said, pointing to a tall, bearded guy who stood shaking his head.

"Isn't that the troubadour?" Jenny asked.

"That's him," Star confirmed. "The second one – the trespasser."

"We don't know anything about that," Jenny argued.

"Let them sort it out."

"Looks like that's exactly what they are doing," Star said.

Jenny and the girls stared as Tyler, the blond guy, put his hands on the bearded guy's chest and pushed. Offering no resistance, the bearded man toppled like a tree and crashed to the ground. Tyler turned around and stalked away without a backward glance. A couple of people in the crowd rushed to help the fallen man.

"That young one has a temper," Star said.

"What do you think they were fighting about?" Betty Sue asked.

"Weren't you paying attention?" Star asked her. "This tall guy is encroaching on that young one's turf. Neither of them is ready to back down."

"I'm beginning to agree with Peter Wilson," Molly said. "Neither of them deserves to be here. We don't need this kind of violence in our town."

Heather was talking to the man called Ocean.

"Are you hurt? Do you need to see a doctor?"

He shrugged off her concern.

"I'm fine. Thanks for asking."

"He shouldn't have hit you," Heather sympathized. "Like you say, the town's big enough for the two of you."

Ocean brushed the dirt off his clothes and shrugged. "He will get what's coming to him."

He thanked Heather again and walked away.

Jenny had gone ahead to order their food. She came out lugging big boxes of pizza and salad. Twenty minutes later, the ladies were at Seaview, Jenny's sea facing mansion, sipping wine and noshing on breadsticks.

"What a day!" Star exclaimed. "The town hall meeting never fails to entertain."

Heather cleared her throat.

"Let's talk about some more pressing things."

Everyone except Jenny nodded their heads.

"This looks like an ambush," Jenny said as she narrowed her eyes.

"Call it whatever you like, sweetie," Star said. "But it's high time we had this conversation."

"We need to start planning your wedding," Molly explained. "Unless you are hiring a wedding planner."

"She doesn't need one," Heather pouted. "She's got us."

"But we are not professionals," Star argued. "We may not be able to come up with a fully coordinated function like a seasoned planner would."

"But I've been looking forward to this since Jenny and Adam became a couple!" Heather cried.

"Relax, you two," Jenny interrupted them. "We are not hiring a wedding planner."

"But why?" Star and Molly chorused.

"I already told you. Adam and I want a small but tasteful wedding. Nothing over the top, nothing too expensive. Hiring a wedding planner is out of question."

"Put me in charge, then," Heather said. "Let me coordinate everything."

"What about us?" Star asked. "We have some ideas too, you know."

Jenny held up her hand.

"You can all share your ideas," she said. "But the final decision is going to be mine."

"Of course, dear," Betty Sue spoke up. "You are the bride, after all."

"Let's start with the date," Heather said. "Fall is almost here. So you will have to be more precise than 'fall wedding'. Pick a date."

"She's right, Jenny," Molly said softly. "How about the first Sunday in November?"

"Weather should be mild enough," Star observed. "Although it could get chilly if there's a winter storm up north."

Jenny gave her approval for the date.

Heather wrote it down in a small notebook she pulled out of her bag.

"This is my official wedding planning notebook. The date's written here now, Jenny. You can't change it."

Jenny popped the lid off a bowl of salad and plunged her fork in. She nodded quietly as she speared an olive and a chunk of feta cheese.

"What about the venue?" Molly asked. "How about the gazebo in town? We can have a marquee in case it rains."

"I would go with the town hall," Betty Sue said. "You don't have to worry about the weather there. And it's got central heating."

"I want a beach wedding," Jenny said. "Do you think that's possible?"

"Have you forgotten you live in a beach house?" Star asked with a laugh. "You can get married right here, on the beach in front of Seaview."

"That's a wonderful idea," Jenny said approvingly. "Let's eat now."

Chapter 3

Jenny was up before the sun the next morning. Dressed in a light summer frock, she set off for the Boardwalk Café at 5 AM. She brewed her first pot of coffee and stood out on the deck, breathing in the cool air laced with a salty tang. The sun crept up the horizon, a large fiery orange ball. Jenny spotted a few early walkers on the beach and waved at them.

By the time Jenny opened the café doors at six, she had baked a few batches of blueberry muffins and brewed some more coffee. Her favorite customer stood on the step outside, ready to barge in.

"Good Morning, Captain Charlie," she greeted him cheerfully. "Ready for your blueberry muffin?"

Captain Charlie took the brown paper bag and large cup of coffee from Jenny.

"That was some meeting last night, huh?" he said. "I was in high school when they elected Mayor Franklin. Can't imagine anyone else in that position."

"I suppose he's getting on," Jenny offered. "Are you thinking of becoming our new mayor?"

Captain Charlie laughed heartily.

"Are you yankin' my chain, missy? I'm ready to hang up my hat. Two more years on the water, tops. You'll find me on the beach in a camp chair with a cooler by my side."

"That's the dream, isn't it?" Jenny sighed.

Jenny stayed busy making crab omelets for the breakfast crowd. The town hall meeting was the talk of the town. Jenny heard snatches of conversation as she went from table to table. The troubadours were a hot topic, so was the mayoral election.

Heather walked in with Betty Sue an hour later.

"Is it 11 already?" Jenny asked as she dabbed her forehead with a tissue.

The ladies went out on the deck and sat at their favorite table. The mid-morning coffee break was a ritual among the friends. They had christened themselves the Magnolias based on Heather's favorite movie. They met every morning come rain or shine, eager to share what was going on in their lives.

Betty Sue pulled out her knitting the moment she sat down. Her needles clacked in a rhythm as she worked on a bright orange scarf. Star pulled out a sketch pad and started doodling. Molly took a book from her bag. Heather was busy tapping keys on her phone.

Jenny placed a plate of warm muffins on the table and took a big bite from one.

"The town's buzzing," she said. "All anyone can talk about are those singers and the election."

"Pelican Cove has always welcomed artists," Betty Sue said, looking up. "There was a really handsome troubadour one year. I must have been sixteen at the time. Lily and I were both smitten."

Lily had been Betty Sue's childhood friend. She had gone missing one night twenty five years ago.

"I don't remember anyone singing songs on the street," Star said.

"We did have a couple of them troubadours when you were new in town," Betty Sue said. "You probably don't remember. But we haven't had any of them traveling singers since Heather here was a teenager."

"I think they are obsolete," Heather said. "Why not just upload a song online?"

"That's a question for Tyler," Jenny said. "Maybe you should ask him the next time you see him."

"Why would I see him again?" Heather scowled. "It's not like I have his number."

"Don't you remember?" Molly asked. "He's got a spot

by the gazebo. You can go over any time you want."

"You can take his picture and put it on that Instagram," Star suggested. "It's one more attraction to draw tourists to town."

"That boy sure is pretty," Betty Sue said, nodding as she twirled a piece of wool over a needle. "I saw you staring at him yesterday, Heather."

"I did no such thing," Heather protested indignantly.

"Hello ladies!" A voice hailed them from the boardwalk.

The Magnolias smiled broadly as a tall, brown haired man walked up the café steps, holding a baby carrier. A bonny baby with large brown eyes clapped her hands as she spotted the women.

"Jason!" Jenny exclaimed. "And Emily. What brings you here this morning?"

Jason Stone was a lawyer, the only lawyer in town. He had recently become a single father. He was juggling work with his parenting duties with plenty of help from his friends. He was in love with Jenny but she had chosen Adam instead.

Jenny sprang up and lifted the baby out of the carrier. The baby grabbed Jenny's hair in her hands and pulled.

"Ouch!" Jenny cried. "You are becoming very naughty, Emily."

Emily cooed and pulled harder.

"She's been doing that a lot lately," Jason said with a grimace.

Everyone wanted to hold the baby. Jenny handed her over to Molly and hugged Jason.

"How about some coffee?" she asked. "It's almost time for lunch."

"Lunch can wait," Jason said seriously. "Haven't you heard yet?"

"Heard what?" the women chorused.

"Did you all go to the town hall meeting?" Jason asked. "I didn't get a baby sitter and Emily was being cranky. So I missed it."

"We were all there," Jenny confirmed. "We know about the election."

"What election?" Jason asked.

"The mayor's election, of course," Heather said. "What are you talking about?"

"I'm talking about the musician," Jason said.

"Something called a troubadour."

"They are traveling musicians," Jenny nodded. "There were two of them."

"What about them?" Betty Sue asked imperiously. "Did they get into another fight?"

"I don't know about that," Jason said. "One of them was found dead a couple of hours ago."

"What?" the Magnolias cried in unison.

"How's that possible?" Star muttered. "They were both very young."

"He didn't die naturally," Jason said.

Emily let out a cry and Jenny rubbed her back, trying to make her stop.

"You don't mean …" she stared at Jason, wide eyed.

Jason pursed his lips and shrugged.

"He was found near the gazebo, strangled to death with a guitar string."

"But who was it?" Heather asked urgently. "Was it Tyler? Or Ocean?"

"I don't know," Jason said. "But I guess you'll know

soon enough. Nothing ever stays hidden in this town for long."

Jason stayed long enough to eat a muffin and have a cup of coffee. Emily ate a few crumbs of muffin that Jenny fed her.

"She already loves your cooking, Jenny," Jason laughed.

Father and daughter bid goodbye and walked down the beach.

"What's wrong with this town?" Betty Sue moaned. "The new mayor needs to focus on crime prevention."

"We don't even have good street lights," Heather pointed out. "And our police force is sadly understaffed."

"Adam's been trying to get the funds for a night patrol," Jenny said. "But the recent budget cuts pushed him to the back of the line."

"But why?" Star asked. "Shouldn't the security of the citizens be the town's top priority?"

Jenny jumped as a shrill voice interrupted them.

"Yooohoooo …"

A short, plump woman huffed up the café steps,

looking full of herself.

"Hello Barb," Betty Sue snapped. "You look like you are about to burst."

"I'm sure you must have guessed," Barb Norton panted.

"Enough with the guessing games," Star drawled. "Why are you here?"

The Magnolias, especially Betty Sue and Star, were always a bit short with Barb. Jenny could never understand why. Barb was at the helm of every project or committee, and she worked tirelessly for the good of the town. But she could be pompous at times. She also took credit for everything she did.

"I'm running for mayor." Barb beamed at them. "I just put my name in this morning."

"We kind of guessed you would do that," Star said dourly.

"That means I can count on your support, right?" Barb asked.

"Who's going to run against you, Barb?" Jenny asked. "I am sure you will be unopposed."

"That's what I think too," Barb said. "But you never

know. This is a democracy, after all. It's a great opportunity to serve the people in this town. Anyone can contest. Even you, Jenny."

"I have my hands full with the café," Jenny smiled. "I don't think I'm qualified, anyway. I don't know the town like you do, Barb."

"What are you going to do to prevent crime in this town, Barb?" Betty Sue thundered.

"We already have a good police department," Barb Norton said. "I thought you would be more interested in promoting tourism, Betty Sue."

"Tourists are great for business," Jenny said. "But they can stretch the town's resources."

Heather spoke up.

"I have a whole list of things we can do to attract more tourists. We can have lifeguards on the beach, for starters."

"What about the library?" Molly asked. "You remember we had talked about allowing tourists to check out books?"

"Hold those thoughts," Barb said. "I'm going to formally announce my candidature soon. There will be a box there for suggestions. Don't forget to drop these in that box."

"What about that dead guy?" Star asked.

Barb Norton had not heard about the dead troubadour. The ladies told her the little they knew. She scurried off, promising to find out more.

Someone struck up a tune on the beach. Jenny shielded her eyes with her hands and peered into the distance. A small crowd had gathered around a tall, bearded fellow. He sang lustily, describing a beautiful woman he had met at a bar.

"That looks like that man called Ocean," Jenny said.

"That means Tyler …" Heather said, her eyes bright with unshed tears.

Jenny patted Heather on the back. There was nothing they could do about it.

The Magnolias dispersed soon after. Star stayed back to help Jenny with lunch. Jenny was quiet as she spooned strawberry chicken salad over slices of bread.

"He was so young," she sighed. "What do you think happened?"

"I don't know, sweetie," Star said. "I hope you are not thinking of getting involved."

"Why would I do that?" Jenny asked with a shrug.

"Adam won't like it," Star warned. "Things are finally coming together for you, Jenny. Don't do something he will frown upon."

"Adam can't dictate what I do," Jenny said. "He knows that very well."

"That's not what I meant," Star said. "Just don't go borrowing trouble. Focus on planning your wedding. Have some fun with your friends."

"Don't worry about me," Jenny assured her aunt. "I didn't even know the guy. Although I do feel sorry for him."

Jenny went to Williams' Seafood Market after she closed up the cafe. Adam was coming over for dinner and she wanted to make something special for him. She got two pounds of shrimp and some fresh sea bass for dinner. Back home, she made her special orange and dill marinade for the fish. She decided to make Adam's favorite tequila lime shrimp along with fresh corn salsa and cilantro rice.

Jenny took a quick shower and dressed simply in a pair of linen shorts and a tank top. Star was already grilling the fish when she went down to the kitchen. Star's beau Jimmy Parsons was also joining them for dinner.

Jenny set the table and lit a few white tapers. She arranged a bunch of fresh roses in a vase. Adam arrived right on time and announced he was starving.

"Tough day?" Jenny asked.

Adam gave a brief nod.

"Any idea what happened to that poor kid?" Jimmy asked.

"We are looking into it," Adam said tersely.

Jenny knew he didn't like mixing his personal life with his professional one. He rarely welcomed any questions related to work, especially any status reports on one of his cases.

"Can you confirm it was Tyler?" Jenny asked meekly.

Adam looked up sharply.

"How do you know his name?" he asked, narrowing his eyes.

"He was at the town hall meeting yesterday," Star explained. "The whole town knew his name, son."

"The victim was one Tyler Jones," Adam said with a sigh. "That's all I can tell you at this time."

Chapter 4

Adam Hopkins sat at a table in the Boardwalk Café, eating a cheese omelet. Jenny topped up his coffee and gave him a secret smile. Adam wasn't fond of showing affection in public, so Jenny resisted planting a kiss on his cheek.

"You're in early," she remarked.

"My shift starts at seven," Adam said. "I thought I might begin the day with a hearty breakfast."

Adam's phone rang just then. He looked sharp as he listened to the voice at the other end.

"I'll be right there," he promised as he hung up.

"What's the matter?" Jenny asked, quirking an eyebrow.

"Nothing for you to worry about," Adam said. "See you later, Jenny."

Jenny watched him hurry out and wondered if it was something related to Tyler Jones. She got her answer soon enough.

The kitchen phone rang just then and Jenny rushed to answer it. Jason Stone's voice came through.

"They just took my client in for questioning," Jason told her. "He swears he is innocent."

"Who's your client? What are you talking about, Jason?"

"It's that troubadour fellow," Jason explained. "He hired me last night."

"Do you mean Ocean?"

"That's the name he goes by," Jason said with a sigh. "I need you, Jenny."

"I don't see how I can help."

Jenny had been involved in solving a few murders in the past couple of years. She wasn't a professional but she managed to get involved for some reason or the other.

"I need to check this guy out," Jason said. "You're the only one I trust."

"I've got a lot on my plate now, Jason," Jenny protested. "Have you forgotten I have a wedding to plan?"

"Just talk to him once," Jason said. "Feel him out. I trust your instincts."

"Adam will flip if I go to the police station now."

Jason paused for a minute.

"You don't have to go there. Let me go and see what's happening there. I'll bail him out if necessary. Why don't you come to my office after we get back? You can talk to him then."

Jenny agreed to talk to the troubadour once he was done with the police.

The Magnolias arrived at their usual time. Jenny placed a plate of truffles before them.

"What's this?" Betty Sue asked suspiciously. "Don't you have anything to eat?"

"Muffins are just coming out," Jenny assured her. "I'm trying my hand at these chocolates. Why don't you try one?"

"You don't have to tell me twice," Heather said as she popped a truffle into her mouth.

She closed her eyes and moaned with pleasure.

"These are so sinful," she crooned. "You have surpassed yourself, Jenny. These are better than your baked goodies."

Molly and Star were also sucking on the delectable

chocolates.

"They just melt in your mouth," Star said. "Where did you learn how to make them?"

"I watched a few videos online," Jenny said modestly. "Then it was trial and error."

"Are you going to sell these in the café?" Betty Sue asked, picking up her third truffle.

"I might," Jenny said. "I'm thinking of making small gift boxes with these. The tourists can buy them as souvenirs."

"I know what!" Heather exclaimed suddenly. "They will make great party favors at your wedding."

"That's a great idea, Heather," Molly said. "We can wrap these up nicely and place them on each table. The guests are going to love them!"

"So you like them?" Jenny asked.

"We love them, sweetie," Star assured her.

"These are made with orange liquer," Jenny explained. "I'm making some with roasted almonds and raisins. And white chocolate."

Jenny was feeling excited. She had created recipes for a

dozen different truffles. She couldn't wait to try them all out.

"Wait till you hear the scoop of the day," Heather said, taking the last truffle from the plate. She paused dramatically until she was sure everyone was looking at her.

"Tyler Jones was a trust fund baby."

"What does that mean?" Molly asked.

"I mean he was loaded. He was richer than any of us can imagine."

"How do you know that?" Jenny asked, her hands on her hips.

"The Pelican Cove grapevine, of course," Heather said. "The masses haven't been idle."

"Why did he sing on a street corner if he had money?" Star asked. "I don't believe it."

"Why shouldn't he?" Heather asked. "It's not like he had to earn a living. I guess he was living his dream, entertaining people with his music."

"Whatever the reason, it didn't end well for him," Molly said seriously.

"They arrested that bearded guy this morning,"

Heather continued.

"You know that too?" Jenny burst out. "How do you find out these things?"

"I have my ear to the ground," Heather said primly. "I'm surprised you didn't know that, Jenny."

"Ocean seemed like a mature guy," Molly said. "Why would he kill Tyler?"

"Turf wars," Heather said matter-of-factly. "Gangs do it all the time."

"Don't be ridiculous, Heather," Star said. "Those two young men didn't belong to a gang."

"But they were fighting for their turf," Heather said. "You were there at the town hall meeting. Didn't you hear what they were saying?"

"Tyler did want to drive Ocean out of town," Molly said slowly. "The opposite happened."

"I think Ocean took care of the problem," Heather said, widening her eyes meaningfully. "He's sly, that one."

"Think before you speak, Heather," Jenny said. "Don't malign someone before you know the whole truth."

"What do you care?" Heather asked, pouring herself a cup of coffee.

"Ocean hired Jason as his lawyer."

"And you are going to help Jason prove his innocence," Heather said. "You better not get too busy for wedding planning, Jenny."

"Relax, I'm just going to talk to him."

"That's what you always say," Star quipped. "And then you end up in a ditch by the side of the road."

"That happened one time," Jenny said. "Ocean seems like a harmless guy."

"A harmless guy who might have strangled someone with a guitar string," Molly reminded her. "I hope you will be careful, Jenny."

The Magnolias joined Molly in expressing their concern. Jenny assured them she would take care of herself.

"Stop!" Jenny held up her hands. "You worry too much. Let's talk about something else."

"Like the fall festival?" Molly said. "They didn't bring it up at yesterday's meeting. Wonder if we are still going ahead with it."

Betty Sue's needles stopped clacking.

"Of course we are," she said. "Pelican Cove takes pride in its festivals. The fall festival will go ahead as planned on the last Sunday in September."

"And we are still having the concert?" Star asked.

"Oh yeah," Heather said breathlessly. "Ace Boulevard is coming to town."

"Ace Boulevard?" Jenny asked. "Aren't they an 80s band?"

"Not just any band, Jenny. They have five gold records to their name. They topped the charts for three years running. Ace Boulevard ruled the eighties."

"But they must be old," Jenny said, scrunching up her face.

"You know the average age of people in this town?" Heather laughed. "They are perfect for us."

"I had cassette tapes of all their albums," Molly said, her eyes gleaming. "This is quite a coup."

"We did say we were going to make a big splash this year," Heather reminded her. "The Bayview Inn is booked solid for the month of October."

"You better start making plenty of these chocolates," Betty Sue told Jenny. "And what about your special menu for the fall festival?"

"I'm still working on it," Jenny said.

"Something with pumpkin?" Molly asked eagerly. "I love pumpkin."

"I do have something in mind," Jenny said evasively. "You'll find out soon enough."

Jenny's phone buzzed and she glanced at the screen quickly. She pressed the talk button and spoke for a couple of minutes.

"Jason wants to see me at his office," she told her friends.

"Go ahead," Star told her. "I'll take care of lunch."

"Thanks, Auntie," Jenny said. "I should be back before that. The sandwiches are ready and so is the soup. The cookies are ready to go in the oven."

"I know the drill, sweetie," Star assured her.

Jenny chose to walk along the beach, enjoying some fresh air as she hurried to Jason's office. It was barely two blocks away. The August sun was hot but the breeze flowing over the ocean made Jenny shiver.

Jason Stone had a visitor.

"You two know each other, right?" he asked, nodding at the tall, bearded man who sat before him.

"I saw him at the town hall meeting," Jenny explained, "but we haven't been formally introduced."

She extended a hand toward the man called Ocean. He shook it and gave her a small bow.

"The police asked him the usual questions," Jason reported. "They let him go now but Adam seems very keen on detaining him."

"I am their top suspect," Ocean said calmly.

"You don't seem worried," Jenny observed.

Ocean shrugged.

"I know I am innocent. The truth will prevail."

"I would try to be a bit more practical," Jason cautioned. "Why don't you tell us something about yourself?"

"That's against the troubadour code," Ocean said. "The troubadour is a man of mystery, an enigma. The only way he communicates with his people is through his poetry and music."

"Man of mystery, huh?" Jenny smiled. "What are you, James Bond?"

"Let's start with your real name," Jason said. "I'm sure the police asked you that."

"My name is Ocean," the man said. "That's exactly what I told the police."

"This kind of attitude will work against you, man," Jason warned. "Where are you from?"

"Planet Earth," Ocean replied. "Any place where the sun shines is my home."

"Where were you born?" Jenny asked. "Are you from around here?"

Ocean had to answer that one.

"I come from a faraway land, the land of the setting sun."

"You mean you are from some place out west," Jenny said. "And you traveled cross country to come to Pelican Cove. Why?"

"I go where the road takes me," Ocean told them. "I don't look at maps or make a plan. I take any turn that takes my fancy."

"So you came here by chance," Jenny summed up.

"That doesn't explain why you are so keen on staying on."

"I like the place," Ocean said. "Is that hard to believe? It's a beautiful town."

"Where did you say you were staying?" Jason asked. "You're not at the Bayview Inn, are you?"

Ocean shook his head.

"Let me guess," Jenny said. "It's against your code to tell people where you live."

"Do you have a phone?" Jason asked. "How will I get in touch with you?"

"I don't believe in being addicted to those death traps," Ocean said. "The radiation from a cell phone can fry your brain."

Jason was looking helpless.

"You will have to be more forthcoming if you want Jason to help you," Jenny warned. "He's a great lawyer but he can't save you unless he has all the facts."

"All you need to know is I didn't kill my fellow troubadour. He was just a kid."

"Why were you fighting with him then?"

For the first time since Jenny had seen him, Ocean looked a bit irritated.

"He pushed me! I almost broke my hip. I walked away without saying a single word."

"Did anyone see him push you?" Jason asked.

"We did," Jenny confirmed. "So did a bunch of other people."

"That's good, I guess," Jason said.

"Good or bad," Jenny reasoned. "People will remember Tyler provoked him."

She turned around to look at Ocean.

"How do we know you didn't go back to get even?"

Chapter 5

"Are you sure you have the right address?" Heather asked Jenny.

The two girls were driving to Richmond to visit Tyler's family.

"It's the one Jason gave me," Jenny said. "I asked Adam to confirm it but he refused to speak about it."

"I bet he's mad you're butting in."

"I'm not," Jenny said. "We are just doing the neighborly thing. We are offering our condolences to a grieving family."

"Stick to that story," Heather snorted. "Why are we going there, exactly?"

"Ocean is the only suspect the police have so far," Jenny said. "I need to find out more about the victim. The logical approach is meeting his family."

"Let's hope they don't drive us out," Heather said grimly.

Jenny entered the city of Richmond and followed directions to Riverside Drive. She had looked it up on the Internet. It was supposed to be a posh area. Houses in the neighborhood cost upward of a million dollars. Nothing could have prepared her for the sight that greeted them though.

A wide drive took them to a plantation house that must have been built in the antebellum days. The stone façade and tall Grecian columns would have impressed anyone. Jenny and Heather stared with their mouths hanging open.

A butler answered their knock.

"We are here to offer our condolences," Jenny spoke up, trying not to be daunted by the inscrutable man towering over her.

"The family is not home for visitors," the butler said dourly.

"We are from Pelican Cove," Heather said. "We saw Tyler the day before he … err, passed."

The butler hesitated before giving in.

"This way please."

He walked down a wide foyer covered in a Turkish carpet and ushered them into a wood paneled room. Tall glass windows channeled in the warm sunlight. Jenny could see the James River gurgling in the distance.

The butler left without a word.

"That's one scary dude," Heather said, laughing nervously.

Jenny motioned her to be quiet.

Half an hour passed without anyone showing up. Jenny had almost decided to get up and leave when she heard someone dragging their feet in the foyer.

A shriveled old man with a shock of white hair shuffled into the room. He wore a three piece suit in a steel gray shade. He flashed a smile at the girls, his gleaming white teeth taking over his tiny face. Jenny guessed they were dentures.

The butler arrived and helped the old man into a wing chair near the fireplace. He made sure he was settled in before leaving the room.

"What brings you here, my dears?" the old man asked in a feeble voice.

A maid came in pushing a trolley loaded with a tea service. She poured tea for everyone and placed a delicate China cup in Jenny's hands. Jenny recognized it was a really expensive brand. Apparently, the Jones family was rich enough to use fine porcelain every day.

Jenny took a sip of her tea and hesitated. The old man gave her an opening.

"You knew my boy Tyler?"

"Not exactly," Jenny said honestly. "He spoke at our town hall meeting. The next day, he was gone."

The old man pulled a white linen handkerchief out of his pocket and dabbed at his eyes.

"He was the joy of my life. He was a good boy. Too young to be taken from us in this manner."

"Jenny's looking into what happened to him," Heather spoke up.

The old man sat up straighter.

"Are you some kind of detective?"

"No," Jenny admitted. "I just meet people and talk to them."

"She's being modest," Heather interrupted. "Jenny has helped solve quite a few murders in our town."

"Find out who killed my boy," the old man said suddenly. "I can pay you whatever you want. I will give you a blank check right now."

"I don't do it for the money," Jenny said, feeling

uncomfortable. "A friend of mine is representing one of the suspects. He wanted me to look into the matter."

"So you just want to collect evidence that proves this man's innocence?" the man asked shrewdly.

Jenny shook her head.

"I want to find out the truth. That's what I do. If Ocean, that's this other man, if he is guilty, so be it."

The man's hand shook as he picked up his teacup and took a sip.

"How can I help?" he asked. "You must have come here for a purpose. What do you want from me?"

"I want to know more about Tyler," Jenny said immediately. "Everything you can tell me about him. Leave nothing out."

"I can do that," the old man said, bobbing his head up and down.

A faraway look appeared in his rheumy eyes. Jenny let him take his time.

"Tyler had a kind heart. He was always doing things for other people."

"Did he always like music?"

The old man's face broke into a smile.

"He started playing the violin when he was six. He began piano lessons a year later. There wasn't an instrument Tyler didn't play. His fingers could create magic."

"He sang too, didn't he?"

"He didn't sing until he was much older," Mr. Jones said. "He joined the choir. He sang like an angel."

"Why didn't he pursue a more traditional form of music career?"

"I don't understand," the old man said, his eyes clouding with confusion.

"You know Tyler was a troubadour?"

"That's a word I haven't heard in decades. You mean those gypsy like singers who go around singing for their supper?"

Jenny nodded.

"Why would my boy do that?" Mr. Jones asked, surprised.

He waved a hand around him.

"He had all this. He could feed a hundred people every day and not feel the pinch."

"Mr. Jones," Jenny said gently. "Tyler came to Pelican Cove as a troubadour. He even applied for a six month permit. He used to stand in the town square and sing all day."

It was obvious Mr. Jones didn't believe them. The tea cup in his hands rattled as his hands shook and his face set in a grimace.

"You wouldn't lie to me, would you? Are you trying to sully my boy's name?"

Heather spoke up in Jenny's defense.

"Mr. Jones, I live in Pelican Cove too. Believe me, we are telling you the truth. Tyler came to our town as a troubadour."

A large young man ambled into the room. His hair was cropped close to his head. His massive belly wobbled when he walked. He flopped down in a chair and spread his legs before him.

"Hey Gramps," he said. "Who are these people?"

"Did you know Tyler sang on the street?" the old man asked the new arrival.

"Must be his latest fad," the man said with a roll of his eyes.

Jenny introduced herself.

"We are here to learn more about Tyler."

"This is my other grandson, Billy," Mr. Jones told her. "He's older than Tyler."

"I'm your only grandson now," Billy said callously.

A golden retriever bounded into the room. A striking pearl and diamond collar glittered around its neck.

"I've seen that dog somewhere," Jenny exclaimed. "She looks very familiar."

"This is Toffee," Mr. Jones said. "She belonged to Tyler. The police brought her over."

"Oh yeah, she was with him that night," Jenny nodded.

She told Mr. Jones about the argument they had seen Tyler have with Ocean.

"Why was Tyler so adamant about not sharing street space?" Jenny asked. "Did he have any old feud with Ocean?"

"Never heard of him," Mr. Jones said. He turned to look at Billy. "Did you?"

Billy picked up a shortbread cookie from the tea cart and munched on it, spilling crumbs on his shirt.

"Tyler was a weirdo. He didn't have any friends."

"You mean he was smarter than you," the old man croaked. "You were always jealous of him, Billy."

Billy picked up another handful of cookies and stalked out of the room.

"Speaking of friends," Jenny said. "Did Tyler have any enemies, anyone who might have disliked him for whatever reason?"

"Billy was right in a way," Mr. Jones said. "Tyler was a quiet one. He spent most of his time making music. He wasn't the kind to hang out at bars and clubs. Most people were attracted to him because of his music."

"But someone must have hated him enough to kill him," Jenny reminded him. "What other motive could anyone have to harm your grandson?"

"What's going on here?" a voice snarled from the door. "Who are these fillies?"

"Mind your manners, Andrew," Mr. Jones bellowed. "These ladies are here to talk about Tyler."

"What do they want? Some kind of donation in his

name?"

"This young lady here is going to find out who killed Tyler."

A tall, balding man wearing an expensive suit strode into the room. He didn't spare a glance toward the women. Jenny guessed the man to be in his fifties. She assumed he was Tyler's father.

"This is my son, Andrew," Mr. Jones said. "He thinks everyone is after the family's money."

"And why shouldn't I?" Andrew Jones demanded. "Someone's here for a handout almost every day."

"We have plenty," Mr. Jones said. "There's nothing wrong with sharing a bit with the less fortunate."

"You sound just like that ninny Tyler," Andrew Jones fumed. "He could have made millions with his music. But he had to go and give it away for free. Singing on some street corner like a beggar!"

"You knew he was a troubadour?" Mr. Jones asked, his eyes wide with surprise.

"What the dickens is a troubadour?" Andrew Jones asked. "All I know is he had pitched his tent in some dingy town on the coast. He stood there in the sun all day, playing his songs on that guitar."

"Why didn't you tell me about this?"

"What's the use?" Andrew asked in disgust. "You would probably have gone and joined him there."

"You didn't approve of your son being a musician?" Jenny asked.

"Tyler wasn't my son," Andrew Jones said in a clipped voice.

Jenny noticed the old man's eyes fill up.

"Tyler was an orphan. His parents died in a plane crash when he was seven."

Jenny didn't know what to say. She muttered something about being sorry.

"You need to leave," Andrew Jones ordered. "My father needs his rest."

"Come back anytime," the old man said hoarsely. "I'm counting on you."

Jenny and Heather walked out under the watchful eye of the butler.

"That was awkward," Heather breathed. "Can't imagine Tyler came from such an uptight family, huh?"

"He didn't have to worry about paying the bills," Jenny

reasoned. "He could do anything he wanted with his life."

"Now we know why he was so stubborn," Heather observed. "He wasn't used to sharing."

The girls drove to Cary Street in downtown Richmond for lunch. Jenny ate her grilled steak sandwich with relish. Heather had chosen the roast duck.

"Have you thought about your wedding gown?" Heather asked Jenny. "I know Molly will have my hide if we go shopping without her, but there's a couple of good shops right around the corner."

"I guess there's no harm in looking?" Jenny asked uncertainly.

"Now you're talking, sista!" Heather gave her a high five.

"One thing's for sure," Jenny said. "I won't be wearing white."

"I guessed as much," Heather said, taking a sip of her sweet tea. "We should have plenty of choices in ivory."

"I don't know how to say this, Heather," Jenny said seriously, unable to hide the twinkle in her eye. "Will you be my maid of honor?"

"Only if you say pretty please," Heather shot back.

The girls clinked their glasses and whooped loudly, their eyes shining brightly.

Chapter 6

Jenny worked the breakfast rush at the Boardwalk Café the next morning. It was a hot and humid summer day in Pelican Cove. The town was flooded with families trying to squeeze in a vacation before school started.

Jenny had placed a box of her truffles at the counter for people to taste. The response was overwhelmingly positive.

"Are you selling these by the dozen?" One woman wearing a gauzy cover-up over her bathing suit asked. "I need to take back some presents for my family. I will take a few dozen of these."

Another man standing behind her was nodding his head.

"I say, that's a great idea. My wife takes care of the shopping but she couldn't come because of a last minute work thing. These will be a nice treat for her."

Jenny beamed at them.

"These are just a sample batch. I haven't decided if I am going to sell them at the café yet."

The woman looked disappointed.

"Why not? They are going to fly off the shelves."

Jenny felt pleased as she put a fresh batch of blueberry muffins in the oven. She was trying to calculate when she could squeeze in an extra hour to make the chocolates.

A tall raven haired man cleared his throat and rapped his knuckles on the counter impatiently.

"Hello Peter," Jenny greeted him.

Peter Wilson wasn't a regular at the café. Jenny was a bit surprised to see him there that morning.

"Wife and kids are away," he muttered. "I need some breakfast. How about a couple of those muffins with coffee?"

Jenny poured coffee in a cup and packed two muffins in a paper bag.

"I guess you heard about Tyler?" she asked.

"Who?"

"That young troubadour," Jenny elaborated. "Haven't you heard what happened to him?"

"Unbelievable, huh?" Peter said without emotion.

"Can I talk to you sometime?" Jenny asked quickly as

she sensed his impatience.

"I need to get back to the garage. Is it important?"

"Sort of," Jenny nodded. "Why don't you grab a table outside? I'll join you in a few minutes."

Peter Wilson grudgingly agreed.

Jenny quickly worked through the rest of the line and went out to the deck with a fresh pot of coffee. A couple of people wanted a top up.

She finally sat down before Peter. He had worked through the muffins and was wiping the crumbs off his face.

"What's the matter?" Peter asked, leaning forward. "You in any trouble?"

"No, no …" Jenny hastened to reassure him. "Everything is fine."

Peter Wilson had been a friend of the café's previous owner. He had kept an eye on her for twenty five years. Jenny guessed he still felt a bit possessive about the café.

"Then what?" Peter prompted.

"I saw you at the town hall," Jenny began. "You seemed pretty riled up."

"You have no idea," Peter grumbled, furrowing his brow. "That kid made my life hell."

"How long was he in town, do you know?"

"He's been banging that guitar for the past four weeks. I thought he would leave in a day or two but he just dug his heels in."

"You didn't like his type of music?"

"I never actually listened," Peter admitted. "I just didn't care for that type of thing. What is this? Las Vegas? We don't want any street performers out here."

"Troubadours have been welcome in Pelican Cove for centuries," Jenny parroted. "At least that's what Betty Sue said."

"He didn't stand outside her window, did he?" Peter shot back. "Now people are making me out to be the bad guy."

"No one thinks you are bad," Jenny assured him.

Peter Wilson hailed from the New Jersey mafia. He had left that life behind when he married a local woman and settled in Pelican Cove. Very few people knew about his past. But it was his Achilles' heel.

"We'll know soon enough," Peter said cryptically,

giving one of his habitual shrugs.

"How's that?"

"I'm going to contest the elections," he smirked. "I could be your next mayor."

Jenny was speechless. She stared at the flannel clad figure before her and tried not to be too judgmental. She knew how snobbish the people in Pelican Cove could be. Peter Wilson was a blue collar worker and an outsider. Would the town people accept a virtual foreigner as their mayoral candidate?

"You don't think I can do it?" Peter asked, narrowing his eyes.

"You'll be up against Barb Norton," Jenny burst out. "Everyone knows her."

"But do they like her?" Peter asked. "She's a bossy old shrew from what I have seen."

"Barb may not have been the mayor all these years," Jenny said carefully, "but she as good as ran the town. She's on every committee, you know."

"The way I see it, it boils down to what this town needs," Peter said seriously. "I am willing to work hard to do that."

"That's admirable," Jenny soothed. "I am sure the

people will appreciate it."

"So I can count on your support?" Peter asked eagerly.

"Sure," Jenny shrugged. "Why don't you work on your manifesto? We can discuss it when you are ready."

"That sounds like a plan," Peter said, slamming his fist on the table. "I knew I could count on you."

Jenny decided to change the subject before Peter got carried away.

"Did you ever see Tyler talking to anyone?"

"What?" Peter asked. "Are we talking about that kid again?" He sounded irritated. "Why are you so hung up on him, Jenny?"

"I am trying to find out what happened to him."

"Are you playing at being a detective again?" Peter asked with a frown. "Just forget that little twerp."

"I can't do that," Jenny said, feeling incensed. "That young man had his whole life ahead of him. He didn't deserve such a gruesome death."

Peter Wilson was looking uncomfortable.

"I guess you are right."

Jenny bottled her own emotions and said goodbye to Peter Wilson.

The day passed in a blur. Jenny had a dinner date with Adam but she was so tired she almost cancelled it. Adam arrived at her doorstep later that evening, holding a long stemmed rose in his hand.

"This is from your garden," he said sheepishly. "I didn't have time to get anything else."

The devil on Jenny's shoulder told her Adam was always busy.

"I have reservations at that bistro you like near Chincoteague," Adam told her. "We need to start right away."

Jenny brushed aside her exhaustion and tried to look upbeat. But her thoughts kept straying to Tyler Jones and his grieving grandfather.

Adam kept up the small talk through drinks and the main course, trying to draw Jenny out. He finally slammed his fork down in frustration during dessert.

Jenny was staring listlessly at her crème brulee.

"Didn't you like the food?" Adam asked. "Why are you so quiet, Jenny?"

"I'm just tired," Jenny admitted. "Summer's always a

busy time at the café."

"And we have double the usual tourists nowadays, thanks to you."

There was a note of pride in Adam's voice. Jenny's delicious food had put Pelican Cove on the map. It had always been a popular holiday destination. But the Eastern Shore of Virginia was lesser known compared to other places in the north. Jenny and her friend Heather had made clever use of social media to advertise the Boardwalk Café and the town itself.

"Do you think the twins will be my bridesmaids?" Jenny asked, referring to Adam's college going girls.

"They will love it," Adam assured her. "I think they are waiting for you to ask them."

Jenny hadn't really given it a thought. She decided to call the girls later.

"You're used to big crowds at the café," Adam mused. "Something else is bothering you."

"Star and the Magnolias are expecting a big wedding."

Jenny told him about having the wedding on the beach. Adam liked the idea a lot.

"So we have the venue," he said cheerfully. "That's a

big item off the list."

Jenny stared at the floor, her eyebrows drawn close in a frown.

"You are not thinking of that dead guy, are you?" Adam asked suddenly. "You have no excuse this time, Jenny. Absolutely no reason to get involved."

"Jason needs my help," Jenny said stoutly. "And Tyler's grandpa wants me to find out what happened."

"Where did you meet that old man?" Adam burst out. "How do you even know that kid's family?"

"Heather and I went to Richmond," Jenny admitted.

Adam balled up his napkin and called for the check. Neither Jenny nor Adam said much on the way back. Jenny stared out of her window and Adam concentrated on getting them home as soon as possible without breaking the speed limit.

"I thought you would be happy planning our wedding!" Adam stomped off after delivering his parting shot.

Jenny tossed and turned all night and was just falling asleep when her alarm went off at 5 AM. She dragged herself out of bed and got ready for the café.

Crab omelets were on the breakfast menu and Jenny

was worked off her feet all morning. Her aunt arrived at 8 to help her out. Jenny felt she couldn't make enough of anything. They were already out of the parfaits she had assembled the previous day. The tourists had gone through four dozen muffins and endless pots of coffee since that morning.

Jenny was feeling harried when Betty Sue Morse barged in, her needles clacking as she twirled white wool around them. Heather was right behind.

"You'll never guess who wants to be mayor," she chortled.

"Peter talked to me yesterday," Jenny said with a smile. "We should support him."

Molly arrived a few minutes later and Jenny joined the Magnolias at their favorite table out on deck.

"I know Barb can be too much," Betty Sue said. "But she's worked hard for the town all these years."

"She's done the time, you mean," Molly said. "But what does she propose to do as mayor? Has she said anything?"

"She is in favor of promoting tourism," Heather told them. "She wants Pelican Cove to be the hottest beach town on the Eastern Shore."

"That's great," Star said. "Good for business."

"Wait a minute," Betty Sue interrupted. "Are you sure more tourists are the answer? The town's resources are stretched already. More crowds mean more litter on the beach, more noise and cars, more pollution…"

"But Grandma," Heather argued. "It's going to be good for our inn. We do well in the summer but our rooms are empty for most of the year."

"We are getting by, aren't we?" Betty Sue said with a shake of her head. "Greed is insatiable."

"You sound just like Peter Wilson," Molly spoke up. "He was at the library yesterday, printing out some flyers. He wants to drive the tourists away."

"That sounds extreme," Jenny offered. "Has he lost his mind? He knows this town runs on tourism."

"He is quoting the dangers of over-tourism," Molly explained. "He is citing the example of European cities like Venice."

"Is the island going to sink because of the tourists?" Jenny sniggered.

"That's not a laughing matter," Betty Sue said, wagging a finger at Jenny. "We can only take so much. It's just never been an issue so far."

"So what you're saying is, thousands of new tourists may not be good for the island?" Heather summed up.

"I think we need a balanced approach," Molly said. "Peter Wilson is incensed because of the troubadours. He is forgetting he himself doesn't belong here."

"That's a bit harsh," Star protested. "He's lived here for twenty five years. And I have lived here for forty five. Jenny here has been here for barely two years. I suppose we don't belong here either."

"That's not what I meant," Molly said, turning red. "I mean Peter Wilson is being unfair, just as he was to Tyler Jones."

Jenny wondered why Peter had taken such a dislike to the young singer.

Chapter 7

Jason Stone swept into the Boardwalk Café, holding a baby carrier in his hands.

"Emily!" Jenny cried as soon as she spotted them. "It's about time you brought her for a visit, Jason."

"This is not a social visit, Jenny," Jason said seriously as Jenny made faces at the baby.

Star heard him as she came out of the kitchen with a fresh pot of coffee.

"Why don't you two sit outside? I can handle everything here."

The breakfast crowd had thinned and Jenny had been ready for a break. She placed some warm muffins on a plate, added a crock of butter and ushered Jason out.

"I bet you missed breakfast."

Jenny nudged the plate toward Jason and put Emily's carrier on the seat next to her. The baby grabbed her finger and wailed heartily. Jenny blew kisses at her and ordered Jason to eat up.

Jason didn't need an invitation. He was already slathering butter on Jenny's banana nut muffin.

"What's got you all hot and bothered?" Jenny asked as she bit into a muffin herself.

"They took Ocean in again."

"What has he done now?" Jenny asked.

"The police searched his van. They found a guitar."

"He's a musician, isn't he? Of course he has a guitar."

"This one had one string missing," Jason said meaningfully.

Jenny's eyes widened as she connected the dots.

"Are you saying this guitar belonged to Tyler?"

"We don't know that for sure," Jason admitted. "But the police think the missing string is the murder weapon. That's why they took Ocean in for more questioning."

"What does he have to say about all this?" Jenny asked, lifting Emily up into her arms as she began to cry.

"Ocean says he found the guitar lying somewhere. He said it looked alright so he picked it up."

"Do you believe him?" Jenny asked, narrowing her eyes.

She stood up and began pacing the floor. Emily stopped crying and grabbed a fistful of Jenny's hair.

"Now you want to play, huh?" Jenny asked in a babyish voice as Emily pulled hard, making Jenny scream in protest.

"Watch out, Jenny," Jason cautioned.

"I'm fine," Jenny assured him. "So do you believe Ocean?"

"Clients always lie in some form or the other," Jason said, starting on a second muffin. "I don't think he's guilty of murder. He could have stolen the guitar, though."

"What do the police have to say about it?"

"You know they found a guitar string on Tyler? They sent it for some forensic testing. Now they will run tests on this guitar too."

"That's it?"

"Things don't look good for Ocean," Jason admitted. "He was already the top suspect. The police are leaning more toward him now."

"You have to defend him because he is your client," Jenny pointed out. "But I don't. I am looking for the truth here. If it turns out that Ocean did it, I will be the first to report him to the police."

Jason nodded as he sipped his coffee.

"I know that, Jenny. I respect your integrity. I won't ask you to do anything you are not comfortable with."

"Thanks, I appreciate that," Jenny told her friend.

Jason Stone had been one of the first people to befriend Jenny when she moved to Pelican Cove. Jenny adored him and didn't want anything to come between them.

"I came here to pick your brain," Jason admitted. "What do I do now?"

"Did you ask Ocean where he found the guitar?" Jenny asked.

"Somewhere on the beach," Jason explained. "He was pretty vague about it."

Jenny waved her hand at the ocean stretching before them.

"You think he can narrow it down?"

Emily had fallen asleep while they talked. Jenny gently put her down in the carrier. Jason had walked to one side of the deck and was waving at someone. Jenny looked up to see a bearded figure ambling along the beach.

"Let's ask the man himself," Jason said, pointing at Ocean. "Looks like the police are done with him."

Ocean climbed up the café steps, looking unruffled. He folded his hands and bowed before Jenny.

"We were just talking about you, Ocean. So they let you go?"

Ocean nodded and sprawled in a chair.

"I am innocent," he said. "Sooner or later, they will realize that. They are free to question me as much as they want until then."

"Why did you pick up that guitar?" Jenny asked him. "And where exactly did you find it?"

"I was planning to hock it," Ocean admitted. "Normally, I would have turned it in, or tried to find out who it belonged to. But there isn't a Lost and Found on the beach, is there?"

He laughed nervously.

"Actually," Jenny corrected. "The town maintains a Lost and Found for all the public beaches. People are leaving stuff behind all the time. Towels, sunglasses, chairs, you name it … sometimes even bathing suits."

"I didn't know that, I swear." Ocean looked contrite for the first time. "I was just looking to make a quick buck."

"It doesn't matter now," Jason said, placing a hand on Ocean's shoulder. "Just tell us where you found the guitar."

"It was on the beach," Ocean said with a shrug. "I already told you that, man."

"You will have to be more specific," Jenny said sternly. "There's miles of beach around us."

Ocean gave them some vague directions.

"What were you doing when you found that guitar?" Jenny asked in frustration.

"I was driving out of town," Ocean told them. "I had a meeting with a fellow in the next town."

Jenny hid her surprise. What was Ocean doing holding meetings with people? It didn't make sense given his zen attitude about everything. She decided to let it slide.

"Go on," she prompted.

"I had to make a pit stop," Ocean said, looking sheepish. "I stopped the car and walked into the beach grass. I saw something shine as I was doing my business."

Jenny tried not to flinch at the image that flashed before her eyes.

Ocean continued.

"What do I see but a perfectly good guitar buried in the sand. I saw dollar signs flashing before my eyes."

"Did you touch it?" Jason asked.

"How else do you think I picked it up?" Ocean quipped as Jason stifled a groan.

The guitar was going to have Ocean's fingerprints all over it.

"Didn't you notice the missing string?" Jenny asked impatiently.

"Not right away," Ocean admitted. "But I wasn't worried. I could easily get it fixed."

"You didn't wonder who the guitar belonged to?" Jenny pressed.

She couldn't believe Ocean was that naïve. Had he really not made the connection with Tyler?

"I didn't give it much thought," Ocean said breezily.

"Finders, keepers."

Jason and Jenny shared a glance. This philosophy was going to cause Ocean a lot of trouble.

"Did you look around?" Jenny asked, wondering if Ocean could help them pinpoint the location.

"You bet I looked around," Ocean laughed. "There wasn't a soul in sight. It was a golden opportunity. I wasn't going to let it pass."

"A golden opportunity for what?" Jenny asked angrily. "Stealing something that didn't belong to you?"

"Calm down, sister," Ocean drawled. "Who said anything about stealing? That thing almost walked into my arms. Some rich dude with too much money must have chucked it without a thought."

"So you didn't see anyone," Jenny said with a sigh. "So no one can vouch for you and tell the police they saw you pick it up."

"Not unless someone from that garage saw me," Ocean said.

"What garage?" Jenny asked sharply. "Do you mean Peter Wilson's auto shop?"

"I don't know," Ocean said. "It's that garage before

the bridge. Someone told me it's the only garage in town."

"You found the guitar on the beach off the bridge?" Jason asked. "Why didn't you say that before, Ocean?"

The bridge connected Pelican Cove to the mainland. It was the only way to enter or leave the town by road.

"Guess I didn't know it was important," Ocean said, scratching his head. "Can I go now? I need to go set up for the day. People expect me to entertain them, you know."

"Go ahead," Jason said.

"You think the bridge is important, don't you?" Jenny said after Ocean left.

Jason looked excited.

"Consider this, Jenny. Whoever ditched that guitar probably drove out of town."

"You are thinking it was someone from out of town?"

"Makes sense, doesn't it?" Jason continued. "Tyler Jones wasn't local. It follows that anyone he knew wasn't from here either."

"It's possible, I guess," Jenny agreed. "But how are you going to prove it? And how will you find this person?"

"I leave that to you, my super sleuth!" Jason teased. "I need to get going. Emily and I have a date at the library."

Jason picked up the baby carrier and set off. Jenny went into the kitchen and started prepping for lunch. She sliced strawberries for her chicken salad and tried to arrange everything she knew about Tyler in a logical order. The Magnolias arrived at their usual time, ready to share some gossip and nosh on something sweet.

"Have you made any more chocolates?" Betty Sue asked her. "I have been craving them all morning."

Jenny shook her head and placed a plate of warm muffins on the table.

"I can barely get through breakfast and lunch. I guess I need to put in some extra time."

"Ask Heather and Molly to help," Betty Sue ordained. "Heather needs to fill her time with something constructive."

"We need to go shopping for your wedding gown," Heather reminded Jenny. "It's a long process and time's running out."

"I know you two looked at some dresses," Molly said with a pout. "Have you already picked something, Jenny?"

"I wouldn't do that without you, Molls," Jenny said quickly. "We just did some window shopping, that too because the store was right next to the restaurant where we had lunch. We couldn't help but look at the display windows."

"Jenny has something to say to you, Molly," Heather said, staring hard at Jenny.

"I do?" Jenny muttered.

She looked bewildered for a minute but she caught on quickly. She grabbed Molly's hand and pulled her to her feet. Then she placed both her hands on Molly's shoulders and beamed at her.

"Molly Henderson, will you be my maid of honor?"

Molly squealed appropriately and hugged Jenny. Heather clapped her hands and Star and Betty Sue followed.

"I'm not done yet," Jenny said. "I want Star to give me away. Molly and Heather, you are both dear to my heart and I don't want to choose between you two. That is why I want you both to be my Maid of Honor. I hope you don't mind sharing."

"We don't," Heather assured her. "But you have to fall in line now, Jenny. Time is short and there's tons of things to do."

"What about Adam's best man?" Molly asked shyly. "Do you think he will ask Chris?"

Chris Williams was Molly's beau. He was a Pelican Cove native and knew Adam well.

"He's not asking Jason," Star said drily, referring to the unspoken rivalry between Adam and Jason.

"Adam's probably forgotten he has to choose a best man," Jenny said.

"Both of you need to start thinking about the wedding now," Heather stressed. "Molly and I are going to take Adam to task."

"Don't forget he's the sheriff, Heather," Jenny said morosely. "He won't rest until he solves this latest case."

"Or you can solve it for him," Betty Sue cackled, looking up from her knitting.

Chapter 8

Jenny walked to the town square after winding up at the Boardwalk Café. She was on a mission. She sat in the gazebo, placed a big frosty cup of sweet tea beside her on the bench and pulled out a book. She leaned back and held the book before her eyes.

Any casual passerby would have assumed Jenny was enjoying a leisurely summer afternoon in the shade. But Jenny had other things on her mind. Her eyes flickered as she took in the space around her. They rested on a bunch of dried bouquets someone had placed below a tree. A sign proclaimed it as Tyler's spot and wished him eternal peace.

A lush green lawn grew around Tyler's spot. There were a few stores bordering the street that ran next to it. The ocean sparkled in the distance. Some houses sat in an alley across an empty parking lot.

A two storied Cape Cod sat on the corner just across where Tyler Jones must have crooned his songs. Jenny assumed it belonged to Peter Wilson. She could see how Tyler's music might have bothered someone living in that house.

An old woman came out of one of the houses and began pottering in her garden. She looked up after some time, spotted Jenny and waved at her. Jenny recognized her as one of the café's regulars.

"Catching up on your reading?" The woman asked in a friendly tone.

"Molly says this is the best book of the year," Jenny replied. "I'm not much of a reader, I'm afraid. I barely have the time."

"That café keeps your nose to the grindstone," the woman nodded seriously. "But you need to take some time off and relax too."

"Music is my relaxation," Jenny offered. "I can't fall asleep without playing some of my favorite records."

The woman bobbed her head emphatically and leaned over the fence.

"Music feeds the soul, doesn't it? I can't imagine life without it … unlike some philistines."

"You mean …" Jenny prompted.

"I just made some fresh lemonade. Why don't you come and have some?"

Jenny finally remembered the woman's name.

"That's kind of you, Trish," Jenny beamed and walked

over to the house.

She admired the roses and the wisteria. Trish looked happy as she ushered Jenny into a small parlor. White lace curtains billowed in the breeze. Chintz covered chairs in a quaint primrose shade faced a pale pink Chesterfield. A large seascape hung over the fireplace and a bunch of photo frames in wood and silver graced the mantel. Jenny recognized the painting as one of her aunt's.

"We bought that from Star a few years ago," Trish supplied. "That was before my Andy passed. He loved that painting. He used to sit right there in that chair and gaze at it for hours."

"I'm sorry," Jenny offered. "You must miss him."

"Only every day," Trish said frankly. "He was the love of my life, you know."

"How do you fill your time now?" Jenny asked with genuine interest.

"I try to keep busy," Trish sighed. "I take care of the garden. We have our share of festivals in Pelican Cove so there's a lot of opportunities for volunteer work."

"Do you have any family in town?" Jenny nodded at the pictures on the mantel.

"The kids all live in the city now. They rarely come to visit. You get used to it. They are busy with their lives, I guess."

Jenny guessed there was a lot Trish wasn't saying. She seemed like a lonely woman.

Trish excused herself and went inside. She came out a few minutes later with a tray loaded with tall glasses of lemonade. There was a plate with chocolate chip cookies.

"Not as good as yours," Trish said generously, offering Jenny the cookies.

Jenny took one and bit into it. She gave Trish a thumbs up.

"These are so good. I might ask you to bake some for the café."

"Really?" Trish perked up. "Do you mean that?"

"I do," Jenny promised. "I am stretched thin at the café. I have been thinking about getting some help. The townsfolk will appreciate something made by one of their own."

Trish regaled Jenny with the different types of cookies she could bake. Jenny's mind drifted as she sipped her lemonade. She didn't notice when Trish changed the subject and started talking about music.

"He was such a nice boy," Trish was saying.

"I'm sorry, who are you talking about?" Jenny asked.

"Tyler, of course," Trish said. "He sang like an angel."

"What type of songs did he sing?" Jenny asked. "Something by Elvis?"

"Tyler wrote his own songs," Trish said with devotion. "He produced his own music too. That guitar just came to life when he played it."

"Did people come and listen?"

Trish nodded vigorously.

"He always drew a crowd. People tipped handsomely too. He made almost twenty bucks in a day."

Jenny thought about the Ferrari sitting in Tyler's garage. Why had he chosen to sing on a street corner in an obscure place like Pelican Cove?

"So he was really popular," Jenny said. "It's hard to believe someone wanted to harm him."

"Not that hard," Trish said, leaning forward. "And you don't have to look too far."

"What are you saying, Trish?"

"You know Peter Wilson, don't you? That car mechanic? He lives right next door."

Jenny nodded.

"He had a big grudge against Tyler. You can say he hated him."

"But why? Tyler's hardly been here a month."

"Said Tyler was disturbing the peace. He used to yell at the poor boy every few hours."

"What did Tyler say?"

"That boy stuck to his guns, said he had a license from the town. He was the troubadour and he was just doing his job."

"But he could have sung his songs anywhere," Jenny argued. "Why did he stick to that spot, knowing he was being a bother?"

"Stubborn, I guess," Trish shrugged. "Or fearless? If someone had threatened me with dire consequences, I wouldn't risk my life."

"You don't think Peter really meant any harm?"

"I hope not," Trish said. "That's the man who wants

to be our mayor."

Jenny tried to give Peter Wilson the benefit of doubt as she drove home. She knew he had a criminal past but he had left it all behind him. Could Tyler's music have driven him to insanity?

Heather and Molly were waiting for her at home. The looks on their faces made Jenny wince.

"You were supposed to be here an hour ago," Heather pounced. "When are you going to start taking this seriously, Jenny?"

"We missed our appointment at the bridal store," Molly clucked.

They had planned to go to a boutique in Virginia Beach. It was owned by a new designer who displayed her latest designs on her website. Heather had sent her the links to some of the dresses and Jenny had really liked them. But they needed an appointment to go try on the dresses.

"I'm so sorry," Jenny apologized. "I ran into someone and lost track of time."

"Were you playing hooky with Adam?" Star asked with a laugh.

She was sitting next to Jimmy Parsons, her special

friend. Jimmy had admired Star from a distance for several years. They had recently reconnected and were taking it slow. Neither of them was in a hurry to take the next step in their relationship.

"I wish," Jenny groaned. "Adam had to attend a seminar in the city. He's going to be late getting back."

"That's good," Heather said. "We need to make up for lost time."

Molly backed her up.

"That's right. Let's start with the guest list. How many out of town guests will you have, Jenny? We will need to make arrangements for their stay."

Jenny's mother hadn't approved of her divorce, even though she had been the victim. She felt everything would be as it was if Jenny just groveled before her ex-husband and asked him to take her back. Relations between mother and daughter had cooled considerably in the past two years. Jenny's mother had declared she was never setting foot in Pelican Cove. Star, who had always been the odd one out in the family, was supposed to be a bad influence on Jenny.

"No one from out of town," Jenny said, knowing her mother would never give her blessing for a second wedding.

Star gave her a sympathetic look.

"Remember, we want it to be small and intimate," Jenny reminded the girls. "Fifty people at the most."

"Fifty people from your side, right?" Heather said. "What about Adam's family?"

Jenny and the girls argued over the list while Star started prepping for dinner. Heather had the first draft of the guest list ready by the time the linguini in clam sauce was ready. Jenny had already poured her favorite Chardonnay for them. Star set the table and dished up the hot, flavorful pasta.

The talk turned to the fall festival.

"Who's going to head the festival committee, now that Barb is running for mayor?" Molly asked.

Barb Norton was an active organizer when it came to town festivals.

"Who says she can't do both?" Heather giggled. "She has enough energy for all of us."

"Why don't you do it?" Jenny asked Star. "It's one of your favorites, isn't it?"

"I'm going to be busy with wedding prep," Star said hesitantly.

"Don't worry about that," Heather said, fanning her mouth. "We got that covered."

"Talk to Barb," Jenny urged her aunt. "I am sure you can convince her to let you take the lead this time."

"I have attended all the meetings," Star said, "so I know what's going on. You are going to love it, Jenny. We took your suggestion from last year. There's going to be a big concert on the beach. We don't really have any space constraints since it will be out in the open."

"That sounds great," Jenny praised. "The Boardwalk Café will provide dessert," Jenny told them. "What about the rest of the food?"

"We are having a big barbecue," Star told them. "Chris and Jason have already volunteered."

"That's what I want for my wedding," Jenny said, feeling inspired. "A barbecue right here on the beach. And a potluck."

"But I already shortlisted a few caterers from up and down the coast," Molly protested. "I was thinking oyster bar, champagne and filet mignon."

Jenny poured some more wine for herself.

"Keep the champagne but ditch the steak. Too fancy schmancy."

"Nothing wrong with having a fancy dinner at your wedding," Heather retorted.

"You forget," Jenny sighed. "I have already done all that."

"Twenty something years ago …" Heather began.

"Whatever," Jenny insisted. "We want something down home and friendly. What could be more coveted than a dish lovingly cooked by our friends?"

"So what? You want corn casserole and potato salad?" Molly wrinkled her nose.

"Adam and I talked about this," Jenny nodded. "We just want your blessings and best wishes. Money can't buy that."

"You don't really need our help, do you?" Heather asked glumly. "You've already got everything figured out."

"On the contrary," Jenny said. "I need you to put it all together for me."

"What about flowers then?" Molly asked, sounding defeated. "I suppose you want roses from your garden?"

Chapter 9

Jenny settled into the plush seat of Jason Stone's fancy car. Even though it was the peak of summer and the air conditioning was on full blast, she was tempted to press the button for the heated seats. There was just something decadent about them.

Jason and Jenny were driving to Richmond. Jenny had received a call from old man Jones. He had suggested Jenny pay a visit to the family lawyer. Jenny didn't know what to expect from the visit so she had asked Jason to go along.

"I really don't see why this lawyer wants to meet us," she said out loud. "I hope it's worth the trip."

"Relax," Jason soothed. "You work too hard, Jenny. Just enjoy your time away from the café."

Jenny tried to follow Jason's advice. She cranked up the radio and enjoyed the view outside the window. They were crossing the Chesapeake Bay Bridge-Tunnel and the Bay sparkled around the long curving road.

They stopped at a rest area on the way. It was too hot for coffee but they both craved a snack.

"How is the wedding prep coming along?" Jason asked

as he handed her a large glass of soda and a cinnamon roll.

"Heather and Molly are immersed in it," Jenny told him. "I couldn't do it without them."

"It's your special day," Jason said gently. "Make sure you don't let them steamroll you."

"They mean well," Jenny said. "Sometimes I think they are more excited about the big day than I am."

Jason pulled up before the offices of Gold, Mason and Arlington a few minutes before 11. The reception area was carpeted in burgundy. It had a look of understated opulence. Jenny guessed most of the firm's clients were as affluent as the Joneses.

A pretty young girl escorted them to a large corner office. A small, wizened man perched in an overstuffed leather armchair, dwarfed by a massive cherry wood desk. He nodded at Jenny and offered his hand to Jason.

"Phineas Gold, at your service."

He offered them coffee and nodded at the girl. She came back a few minutes later, carrying a tray with a silver coffee urn and delicate mugs. Jenny accepted a cup and thanked the girl.

"Thanks for driving all the way to town," Phineas Gold began. "I suppose you are wondering why I called you here."

Jenny nodded as she took a sip.

"The Jones family has a long association with the firm. Josiah's father hired my great grandfather sometime in the 19th century. We have taken care of their legal affairs since then."

Jenny had a lot of questions but she let the man continue.

"Josiah told me you are looking into Tyler's death for him. I have some information that might be relevant to you."

Jenny sat up in her chair, feeling hopeful.

"You know Tyler's parents died when he was young. He was their sole heir. All the money was tied up in a trust until he reached twenty five."

"When was he coming into this trust?" Jason asked.

"This week," Phineas said meaningfully.

Jenny was two steps ahead.

"Who gets the money now?" she asked.

"Tyler could have left it to anyone, but he didn't have a will. He ignored our professional advice and never made one. Said it made him feel morbid."

"He was barely twenty five," Jenny whispered. "Of course he didn't think he needed one."

Phineas Herb looked impatient.

"Tyler's parents did think of this scenario though. They left everything to Tyler's uncle."

Jenny remembered the tall, rude man she had encountered at the Jones residence.

"Doesn't he have a son too?"

Phineas nodded.

"It will all go to him, eventually. But Tyler's uncle gets it for now."

"Did Tyler get along with his uncle?" Jenny asked. "I had the impression he didn't approve of Tyler's music."

"Tyler wasn't interested in the family business," Phineas told them. "It was a source of friction between him and his uncle."

"What about old Mr. Jones?" Jenny asked.

"The Jones family is loaded. Tyler could live in the lap of luxury without having to lift a finger. The old man just wanted him to be happy."

"Isn't this all kind of personal?" Jason asked. "I'm surprised you are telling us all this."

"I am acting on my client's instructions," Phineas Gold grumbled. "I don't see how this is going to help you find Tyler's killer."

"It opens up a line of investigation," Jenny told him. "Tell me, what is your opinion of Tyler's uncle?"

Phineas Gold looked scandalized.

"I don't gossip about my clients, Madam."

"Was he short of funds?" Jenny asked doggedly.

Jason caught Jenny's eye and gave a slight shake of his head. The old man must have pressed some kind of button. The pretty young girl came in and started to show them out.

"Tyler may not have been practical but he was kind," Phineas said as they were leaving. "I hope you find out who murdered him."

Jason knew Jenny liked Chinese food. He drove to a local restaurant tucked away in a strip mall.

"Save room for dessert," he told Jenny. "Their fried banana fritters are not to be missed."

They ordered a generous lunch and began eating with gusto. Jenny deftly picked up a steamed dumpling with her chopsticks and looked at Jason speculatively.

"What was the whole point of that visit?" she asked. "Does the old man want us to suspect his son?"

"I've been wondering that myself," Jason said, scrunching his face.

"Money is always a strong motive," Jenny said. "And the uncle didn't seem too fond of Tyler."

"Shouldn't the uncle be rich in his own right, though?" Jason asked.

"He might have needed the money for a secret project," Jenny pointed out.

"So what?" Jason scoffed. "He bumped his nephew off? It sounds farfetched."

"You know who else is beginning to look like a suspect?" Jenny asked. "Peter Wilson."

"Come on, Jenny, Peter can be hot headed. But you don't seriously think he's guilty?"

"He hated Tyler and had several confrontations with

him," Jenny reminded Jason. "And he even threatened the poor kid."

"That still doesn't mean he did it."

"We don't have any other suspects," Jenny muttered. "Unless you want to consider Ocean."

"What does Ocean gain by getting Tyler out of the way?" Jason asked.

"He's the sole troubadour in town now. That seemed important to him."

"You're getting mixed up," Jason said, shaking his head. "Tyler is the one who wanted to drive Ocean out."

"Whatever," Jenny shrugged. "Ocean is the only entertainer in town now. He gets to rake in the moolah."

Jason laughed at that.

"So he earns twenty bucks more than he would otherwise. Not a strong enough motive to kill someone."

Jenny stared moodily at her Sichuan chicken.

"I'm completely out of ideas," she admitted.

"What does Adam say about all this? The police must be doing something other than harassing Ocean?"

Jenny rolled her eyes.

"You know Adam doesn't like talking about his work. He's already warned me to leave this alone."

"He's not completely wrong," Jason considered. "You are about to be a bride. Enjoy all the pre-wedding fun, Jenny. Forget all this running around."

"But you're the one who wanted help with Ocean," Jenny reminded him.

Jason slapped his forehead.

"Guilty as charged. But you've been a big help so far. I don't think there is any hard evidence against Ocean."

"So you want me to drop all this?" Jenny asked, scraping the last bit of fried rice off her plate. "It's not that easy. And I promised old Mr. Jones I would look into it."

"I think you've done your bit," Jason said with a sigh. "Forget all this for now. Let's order dessert."

Jason mentioned the wedding again on their way back to Pelican Cove.

"Where are you going to live after the wedding?"

Jason knew Jenny was very fond of Seaview, the beach facing mansion she had bought with her divorce settlement. She had clearly expressed she didn't want to live anywhere else. Adam was equally adamant about his own house. Jenny's friends had secretly started a pool about where the couple would live after they got married.

"We are still talking about it," Jenny divulged. "But Adam will come around."

"Now this wouldn't have been a problem if you were marrying me," Jason joked.

Jenny knew the remark was only half in jest. Jason had made it clear he would follow Jenny to the end of the world if needed. Everyone wondered why Jenny had chosen Adam instead of Jason. But as they said, love didn't always follow logic.

"Emily's growing up real fast, isn't she?" Jenny asked glibly.

Betty Sue and Heather were watching Jason's baby for the day. Jason's hands tightened on the steering wheel.

"Am I doing right by her, Jenny?" he wondered out loud. "A baby girl needs her mother. Do you think I should get married?"

"What are you planning to do? Order a wife online?"

Jenny scoffed. "Don't be silly, Jason."

"That's not what I meant," Jason murmured.

"If you are thinking about dating again, I think you should go ahead. You don't lack baby sitters. We will gladly take care of Emily while you go out."

"You think anyone will want to date a single father like me?" Jason asked, his doubt splashed clearly across his face.

Jenny gave him an encouraging smile and began to check off his attributes on her fingers.

"You are a successful lawyer, you own the house you live in, you are not bad on the eyes, and you have a heart of gold … wait a minute, you have a lovely baby girl. You, my dear, are a great catch!"

"If you say so, Jenny," Jason mumbled.

Jenny tried to cheer Jason up. She fiddled with the radio and tuned into Jason's favorite station.

"You like Springsteen, don't you?"

They both sang their hearts out to 'Born in the U.S.A'. Jenny broke off as Jason turned onto the bridge leading to Pelican Cove.

"What in the world!" she exclaimed, pointing to a large

billboard.

Barb Norton's face stared back at them, flashing a 1000 mega watt smile. 'Barb Norton for Mayor', proclaimed the large letters splashed across the poster.

"Barb does everything in style," Jason laughed. "She's going to win in a landslide."

"I wouldn't be so sure," Jenny said as Jason drove off the bridge.

She pointed toward the side of the road.

Peter Wilson's auto shop was festooned with hundreds of balloons. Music played in the background and a small crowd had gathered. Jenny spied people holding small paper cups of lemonade. A line of cars snaked along the road leading to the garage. A car wash event was in progress. High school kids were busy cleaning the cars while the guests mingled. Peter Wilson could be seen moving around, shaking hands.

"Looks like Peter has upped his game too," Jason remarked.

"Election canvassing is on alright," Jenny said as they drove further into town.

Lawn signs had gone up before most of the houses. Jenny counted the election placards and tried to calculate who was leading the race.

"Barb may be a busybody but she has done a lot for this town," Jason said. "She definitely has my vote."

They came upon another crowd as they drove up to the town square. Barb stood in the gazebo, getting ready to give a speech. People waved tiny American flags and cheered her on.

"What is Peter offering to do anyway?" Jason asked.

"He's going to put a stop to over-tourism," Jenny said, putting double quotes around the word. "He doesn't want the town to change too much."

"You mean he's against growth?" Jason frowned.

"I'm sure he doesn't see it that way," Jenny replied.

Jenny's phone rang then. She stared at the unknown number, then made up her mind and pressed the green button. She spoke briefly before hanging up and stared at Jason meaningfully. He had just pulled up before Jenny's home.

"That was old Mr. Jones," she said in a hushed voice. "He wants to see me again."

Chapter 10

Jenny bustled about in the Boardwalk Café, chatting with customers and topping up coffee. The sun shone brightly outside, and the beach behind the café was packed with sun worshippers and families enjoying summer vacation. Most of the townsfolk were out too, canvassing for their favorite mayoral candidate.

The café crowd thinned after a while and Jenny finally went back inside to prep for lunch. Her strawberry chicken salad was so popular she was making gallons of it every day. Soft shell crab season was on and it was another item Jenny couldn't make enough of.

"You look tired," Star observed as she drained the poached chicken.

"I'm fine," Jenny muttered without looking up.

She had sliced a mound of strawberries and was ready to start mixing the salad.

"You need to take better care of yourself," Star droned. "Can't have you looking like a hag on your wedding day."

"Why does everything come around to that nowadays?" Jenny complained.

Star just shook her head quietly, opting not to say anything.

"Tell you what," she said after a few minutes. "Why don't you go out for lunch? Take a picnic basket and meet your young man."

"Adam's going to be busy," Jenny said with a grimace. "I don't think he can spare the time."

"Nothing wrong with asking," Star said. "Better yet, go surprise him and ask him sweetly. I am sure he won't be able to say no."

The Magnolias arrived at their usual time.

"You need to ask Adam about his guest list," Heather reminded Jenny.

Jenny promised she would do that when she met Adam later.

"Mandy is in town," Molly informed them. "I saw her going door to door with Barb as I was coming here."

Mandy was a publicist the town hired from time to time. She had been instrumental in modernizing a lot of things in town. She could be pushy but Jenny admitted Mandy had helped spread the word about the Boardwalk Café. Tourism had boomed in town since Mandy's arrival.

"Barb must have hired her for the election," Betty Sue observed, her hands busy knitting an orange scarf.

"Does that mean she won't be helping with the fall festival?" Star grumbled. "I was counting on her assistance."

"Why don't you ask her?" Jenny asked, pointing in the distance. "I bet those two ladies are on their way here."

The Magnolias looked up from their coffees and muffins and stared at the beach. Two familiar figures were hurrying along the sand, weaving their way around people lying on towels or lounging in camp chairs under colorful umbrellas.

"Yoohoo …" Barb Norton called out her signature greeting and waved at them.

She huffed up the steps a few minutes later, trying to catch her breath. Mandy was at her heels, holding a pen and notepad in her hands.

"Looks like you are painting the town red, Barb," Betty Sue cracked.

"I believe in a job well done," Barb said pompously. "You know that about me, Betty Sue. I have always taken care of this town. I will continue to do so when I become mayor."

"You are that confident of winning, huh?" Star quipped.

"Of course I am going to win. People like you fully support me and can't wait for me to be mayor."

She gave them a speculative look.

"I can count on your vote, right?"

"What do you propose to do for the town?" Betty Sue asked. "I need to know you won't turn this place into a circus. Jenny here said you are angling to bring more tourists down here?"

"Of course!" Barb beamed. "Boosting tourism is one of the top items on my agenda. We need the money these people bring in. Most of the businesses in town depend on tourists, Betty Sue. Your own inn needs them."

"That doesn't mean you should flood the town with these folks."

Barb Norton looked flustered.

"Why don't you just come out and say it, Betty Sue?" Barb thundered. "You want to vote for that chicken necker Peter Wilson."

"He is talking about preserving our heritage," Betty Sue said stoutly. "This is the land of my ancestors,

Barb Norton! I don't want to see it sink because you brought in a boat load of outsiders."

The two women continued to bicker over the issue. Jenny, Heather and Molly looked at each other and tried to suppress their smiles.

Star took Mandy to task.

"Can I still count on your help for the fall festival?"

"Don't worry," Mandy said smoothly. "I am working on a presentation for our next meeting. Everything is running on schedule. Barb told me you are heading the festival committee now?"

"That's right," Star said proudly. "And I want everything to go off without a hitch."

"The concert is going to be big," Mandy told her. "That itself should help us reach our fundraising goal."

"What about games and rides?" Star asked. "Hay wagon rides are absolutely must. And people expect the usual contests like pumpkin carving, best yard decorations and so on. Are you keeping track of that?"

Mandy reassured Star she had everything under control.

"For shame, Betty Sue!" Barb roared suddenly,

springing up. "I didn't expect this from you."

"What's wrong with having a debate?" Betty Sue asked with a frown. "It's what happens in every election."

Barb was breathing fire as she clattered down the steps without a word.

"Now you've done it, Betty Sue!" Star drawled. "Did you have to rile her up?"

"Did you see her?" Betty Sue cackled. "She got as red as a tomato."

The Magnolias chattered for a while longer. Heather reminded Jenny of plenty of wedding related chores before they left.

Jenny went into the kitchen and started assembling a picnic basket. She added chicken sandwiches, chips and Adam's favorite chocolate chip cookies. Two bottles of lemonade went in along with some truffles Jenny had made that morning.

"Don't forget a blanket," Star called out.

The noon sun felt scorching as Jenny walked to the police station. She was glad she had remembered to wear her straw hat. The breeze coming off the ocean offered some relief from the heat.

Adam's face lit up when Jenny peeped into his office.

"Jenny! What a nice surprise!"

"Can you get away for lunch?" Jenny asked, holding up the picnic basket before him.

"Why not?" Adam said with a shrug. "I need a break from these files. And I'm starving."

Adam picked up his cane but Jenny noticed he didn't lean on it much. Adam was a war veteran who had been injured in the line of duty. She knew he was trying hard to get rid of the cane for their wedding. It was supposed to be a surprise for her so she didn't make any comment.

They walked out and strolled to the beach. Jenny pointed to a spot and Adam spread the blanket in the sand.

Adam guzzled the cool lemonade before picking up his sandwich.

"What's new at work?" Jenny asked.

"The usual," Adam said between bites. "Nothing worth talking about."

"Is it always going to be like this?" Jenny bristled. "When are you going to learn to trust me?"

"What do you want to know, Jenny?" Adam asked

with a sigh. "Is this your way of digging for information?"

"I'm not always doing that," Jenny snapped, putting a half eaten sandwich down.

"Are you still helping Jason?" Adam asked sternly. "Tell me you don't care what happened to that kid."

"I can't," Jenny said. "An innocent young man was struck down in the prime of his life. I can't just forget about that, Adam, especially when the police don't seem to be doing anything about it."

"There you go again," Adam muttered.

"Do you have any new leads?" Jenny asked. "The only two suspects we have are Peter Wilson and the uncle."

"Uncle?" Adam asked.

Jenny told him about the trust fund.

"You never cease to amaze me, Jenny."

"Is Ocean still at the top of your list?" Jenny asked. "Or do you have any other evidence."

"The guitar came back from forensics," Adam told her. "There were three sets of fingerprints on it. We identified two of them as belonging to Tyler and Ocean."

"What about the third set?" Jenny asked eagerly.

"Unknown."

Jenny's eyes widened as she processed this latest piece of information.

"Could it be Peter Wilson?" Jenny mused. "Ocean told us where he found the guitar. It was just off the bridge near Peter's garage. He could easily have thrown it there."

"What would Peter be doing with that guitar?"

"He was known to have shouting matches with Tyler. He found Tyler's music offensive. Maybe he grabbed the guitar sometime in a fit of anger."

"Believe it or not, we thought of that," Adam said drily. "Peter's prints are already on file."

"So it's someone other than Peter?"

Jenny didn't hide her relief. Peter Wilson had always been good to her. She thought he hadn't behaved well with Tyler. But she didn't want to believe he had actually harmed the boy.

"As of now, we have no idea who those prints belong to."

"Try matching those prints with Tyler's uncle."

"Tyler and his uncle lived in the same house, right? So any of his family could have touched that guitar. I am surprised we found only three sets of prints."

"I bet it was someone Tyler knew from out of town."

"Enough of all this, Jenny," Adam said. "Stop pumping me for information. I don't have anything else to tell you."

Jenny smiled coyly as she offered Adam some cookies.

"Have you worked on your guest list?"

Adam looked sheepish.

"I haven't had the time. But I think you already covered anyone I want to invite."

"How is that possible?" Jenny asked. "What about your family or friends from the military?"

"Most of my family are gone," Adam explained. "The rest are relatives of my first wife. I don't think it's appropriate to have them here for our wedding."

"And your friends?" Jenny asked.

"Some are still deployed. Some aren't around anymore."

"I'm sorry," Jenny mumbled as she worked out what Adam meant. "So it's just you and the girls and your brother?"

"We don't need too many people, Jenny," Adam said, holding her hand. "Just a few close friends and their blessings."

"What about your suit? You are not getting out of wearing a tux, mister!" Jenny said sternly. "No shorts or floral shirts."

"Why not?" Adam teased. "Aren't we getting married on the beach?"

"Don't let Heather hear you say that," Jenny warned. "And you need to ask Ethan to be your best man, unless you have someone else in mind."

Adam assured her he would get all that done. Adam wanted to get back to work. Jenny offered him the chocolates she had made earlier.

"Something for your 4 PM sugar rush," she smiled.

Jenny swung her basket from side to side as she took the scenic route back to the café. She wondered if Adam was being sufficiently enthusiastic about their wedding. How could he not have any guests of his own? Then she dismissed her thoughts as being obsessive.

Had Heather's constant nagging finally turned her into a bridezilla?

Chapter 11

A low hum of conversation rippled across the dimly lit pub. The Rusty Anchor had provided sustenance to the locals since 1879. The Cotton family and its descendants had been running it proudly since days of yore, when Pelican Cove had been Morse Isle.

Jenny and her friends had decided to gather for drinks that evening. Jason had squeezed an hour out to be with them, reluctantly letting Betty Sue and Star watch Emily.

"This is nice," Heather said, sipping a glass of wine. "I don't remember the last time we all got together like this."

Jenny stared moodily into her own glass of wine. Adam was working late again and wasn't going to join them. She tried not to be jealous of Molly and Chris, standing close together with their arms around each other. Her relationship was different and she would have to get used to it.

Eddie Cotton came over to their table with two large mugs of beer. He set them on the table and stopped to chat with them.

"You are not going to some fancy city pub for your

drinks, are you? It's been a while since I set eyes on you."

"Of course not," Heather said cheerfully. "Everyone is just too busy."

She pointed toward Molly and Chris.

"These two love birds can barely spare a glance at anyone else. Jason's busy with the baby, as he should be. Jenny's swamped at the café. And I am the official wedding planner for the wedding of the year."

"What's that music you are playing, Eddie?" Jenny asked. "Sounds captivating."

"That's the poor kid who got bumped off," Eddie said.

Jenny sat up straighter.

"How do you have his music?"

"He gave it to me … he had to cut something, he said."

"He cut a disc for you?" Heather prodded. "That was nice of him."

"Came here every night after he wound up for the day," Eddie told them. "Had a beer."

"So you knew Tyler well?" Jenny asked eagerly.

Eddie shrugged.

"We talked a bit. He was loaded, you know. He tried to hide it but I knew he came from money the moment I laid eyes on him. Drove here all the way from Richmond every day."

Jenny was surprised Eddie knew so much about Tyler's background. She wondered what else he had shared with Eddie.

"He was a shy one," Eddie said, anticipating her questions. "Sat in a corner over there and barely spoke to anyone."

"Surely the locals must have recognized him?" Jenny asked.

Eddie scratched a spot on his face and pursed his lips.

"He sat facing the wall. He made it clear he wanted to be left alone."

"How did you know who he was?" Jenny asked.

"I saw him singing in the town square, didn't I?" Eddie puffed up. "My missus heard him first. She was a big fan. She took me there to listen to this guy. Didn't believe me when I told her he had a beer at our pub every night."

The group plunged into an animated discussion about the upcoming elections.

"Peter Wilson may turn out to be a dark horse," Jason said seriously. "Nothing wrong with having someone new at the helm, of course. He will keep everyone on their toes."

"I think Barb will pack her bags and move to Florida if she doesn't win the election," Heather chortled. "She wouldn't be able to handle the shame."

As everyone in town knew, Barb Norton's daughter lived in Florida. Barb was a snowbird, spending every winter with her daughter down in the sunshine state.

"She won't give up that easily," Molly said thoughtfully. "And why should she? She has toiled hard for this town."

"So you are in Barb Norton's camp?" Jenny asked her.

Molly looked uncertain.

"I don't know, Jenny. Part of me feels I should be loyal to Barb."

"It's not a question of loyalty," Chris Williams spoke up. "It's just an election, for heaven's sake."

"You poor sod," Heather laughed. "It's never 'just' anything. I guess we were better off with that old fogey for mayor."

"Now that I don't agree with," Jason said strongly. "Anything is better than that. Both Barb and Peter seem fired up to do some work. Whoever gets elected, they will finally be taking action. We might even get parking meters on Main Street."

Heather punched Jason in the shoulder.

"No parking meters! We are not that evolved yet. Don't go spouting these crazy ideas, Jason."

"What's wrong with having parking meters?" Jason asked, rubbing his shoulder dramatically. "Ouch, Heather, you do pack a mean punch."

"Parking meters are a blot on our rustic charm," Heather stated, draining her wine.

"Stop squabbling, you two!" Molly reproached them.

She nudged Heather and tipped her head toward Jenny. Jenny was absently twirling her wine, staring in the distance.

"What's eating you, Jenny?" Molly asked solicitously. "You know you will meet Adam in a few hours, right?"

"You love birds!" Heather sighed, rolling her eyes.

"She's going to get worse," Molly said. "I bet she's dreaming about the wedding."

Heather grew alarmed when Jenny didn't call them out.

"Are you okay, Jenny?" she asked, coming around to hug her friend. "What's the matter with you?"

Jenny's eyes were bright with emotion.

"I was thinking about Tyler," she admitted. "All my efforts have been futile. I have never felt so helpless."

"You just haven't talked to the right people," Jason soothed.

"Tyler was popular, right?" Jenny said with exasperation. "He must have talked to someone other than Peter Wilson?"

Chris let out an exclamation.

"I just remembered … that kid was talking to someone in a fancy car."

"You mean like a limousine?" Jenny asked eagerly.

"Way more expensive," Chris said. "Like a Porsche or a Ferrari. Something that costs six figures."

"Which one was it exactly?" Jenny prompted.

"I couldn't say," Chris apologized. "I wasn't really paying attention. I noticed it because it was red and shiny and low slung. No one in Pelican Cove owns such a car, at least as far as I know."

"Tell me more," Jenny said urgently. "Did Tyler get into the car? Did anyone get down from it? What were they talking about?"

"How would I know, Jenny?" Chris asked. "I spotted them from a distance."

"Think harder, Chris."

Chris was shaking his head and shrugging his shoulders when he exclaimed again.

"Looked like a heated discussion. Tyler didn't look too happy."

"Are you sure you are not making this up?" Molly asked.

"To be honest, I don't remember much," Chris admitted. He looked at Jenny and winced. "Sorry, I guess?"

Jenny waved off his concern.

"Don't worry about it. How about another drink? This round's on me."

Molly and Chris stayed for a while and then said goodbye. Molly had cooked a pot roast and they were both looking forward to a cozy dinner at home.

Heather took her leave next.

"Don't worry about Emily," she told Jason. "Her Auntie Heather will look after her until you get back."

Jason had switched to water after one beer.

"I just want to talk to Jenny for a bit," he said. "I'm right behind you."

"Why don't we walk to the Bayview Inn?" Jenny suggested some time later. "We can talk on the way and I can say hello to Emily."

"What's really bothering you, Jenny?" Jason's voice was full of concern as he peered at Jenny in the dark.

The waning moon was a thin sliver and the inky sky was studded with stars. Jenny still couldn't help marveling at them. She had barely noticed them when she lived in the city. Now she reveled in the beauty that surrounded her, right from the thundering ocean right outside her house to her lush garden.

"When will you stop worrying about me, Jason?" she asked softly.

"Never," Jason declared vehemently.

He made no attempt to hide his fervor. For the first time, Jenny wondered if she had chosen the wrong man.

"Adam's a cad," Jason exclaimed, as if reading her mind. "Is he really so busy?"

"He's taking a week off after the wedding," Jenny said meekly. "We are going to drive north to Maine, to Acadia National Park. I have never been there."

"At least he's planning a honeymoon," Jason conceded.

"He can't shirk his responsibilities," Jenny said staunchly. "Being sheriff comes with its own burden."

"Speaking of which … does he know about this man in the car?"

"Adam doesn't exactly swap notes with me, Jason. You should know that by now."

"Maybe you should tell him."

"You think this man is important? He could just have been a tourist, asking for directions."

"Don't forget the third set of prints," Jason reminded her.

"That's a long shot," Jenny said, turning around to face Jason. "And how are we ever going to locate this guy? We don't even know his name."

"I suppose you can't ask your customers if they saw a fancy red car?" Jason joked.

"If you ask me, that car is long gone. So are any tourists who might have been in town around that time."

"You're right, Jenny," Jason nodded. "I'm just grasping at straws. Ocean is still the prime suspect. Funnily enough, he doesn't seem to be too bothered about it."

They reached the Bayview Inn and Jason rushed in to gather his daughter in his arms. Jenny wanted to hold her next. She cuddled the baby and breathed in her special baby smell. Emily grabbed her hair and pulled hard.

"Stop that, Emily," Jason said in a stern voice, trying to pry her fingers apart.

"She's a feisty one," Betty Sue laughed, looking up from her knitting. "She's going to lead everyone a merry dance."

Jason put Emily in her carrier and said goodbye to the ladies.

"I didn't expect you to be here," Jenny said to her aunt.

"Betty Sue was craving my lasagna," Star explained. "So I made a pan and brought it over. We are eating here tonight. Is that okay with you, honey?"

"No complaints from me," Jenny laughed, "as long as I have a couple of slices of your special lasagna."

"You better eat up," Heather said purposefully. "We have our work cut out after that."

"More wedding chores?" Jenny groaned. "Can't we have a night off, Heather?"

"Not tonight," Heather said firmly. "We need to finalize the invitations. You need to send 'save the date' cards at the very least."

"You sound like a sadist," Jenny said viciously. "You get some perverse pleasure from all this, don't you?"

Heather's eyes filled up.

"Am I being too hard on you?"

Jenny rushed to console her friend.

"You are the best wedding planner a girl could possibly have, Heather."

"Come on, you two," Star called out. "Dinner's getting cold."

"Let's look at the designs you shortlisted after we eat," Jenny promised Heather.

Jenny pushed all thoughts of Tyler from her head and went in to have dinner with her friends.

Chapter 12

The stifling heat of the summer had finally receded. The lower humidity put a smile on everyone's face. The Magnolias sat on the deck of the Boardwalk Café, sipping iced coffee and trying out Jenny's latest batch of truffles.

"White chocolate and orange liquer," Heather moaned in pleasure. "This is my favorite so far."

Molly shook her head.

"I think orange works better with dark chocolate."

"I am making both," Jenny told them. "People either love white chocolate or don't. It's mostly butter, though. Not as healthy."

Betty Sue looked up from her knitting and peered at the beach.

"I thought I heard that woman," she muttered.

Betty Sue seemed to have a sixth sense when it came to Barb Norton. Barb and Mandy came up the beach, looking flustered.

"What's up, Barb?" Star asked. "You look like a child

who's lost his favorite toy."

"Ladies," Barb said heavily, collapsing in a chair. "We have a crisis on our hands."

"Someone else is contesting the elections?" Heather asked.

"This is about the fall fest," Mandy corrected her. "You remember that 80s band that was going to headline our concert?"

The Magnolias nodded with varying degrees of interest.

"They pulled out," Mandy said grimly.

"Wait a minute," Star said. "Does Barb know about this?"

"Of course I know," Barb said. "Why do you think I'm here?"

"Why does Barb know and I don't, Mandy?" Star roared. "I am the head of the fall festival committee. Anything goes wrong with the festival, you come to me first."

Mandy stared at Star, her mouth hanging open.

"Stop acting like a child, Star," Barb snapped. "How does it matter who she goes to? She did the right thing coming to me."

"No she didn't," Star said stoutly. "You handed me the reigns of the festival committee. Or have you forgotten already?"

"Yes, yes," Barb said impatiently. "We all know who's running the show. But aren't you missing the point, Star?"

"Stop this nonsense, you two," Betty Sue spoke up. "You can figure out who comes first later. We have a problem on our hands."

"Didn't you have a contract with that group?" Heather asked Mandy. "I thought you take care of things like that."

Mandy shook her head.

"We were in the process of doing that. It appears that this band is going on tour with someone. It's a much more lucrative deal for them than a small town festival."

"So what?" Star grumbled. "They just abandoned us?"

"They have apologized," Mandy offered. "The lead singer says he is really sorry he has to pull out at short notice."

"A fat lot of good that's going to do us," Betty Sue said with a frown.

"You should have come to me first," Star said to Mandy. "Why don't I try talking to him once?"

"You think I haven't done that?" Barb asked. "It's no use. They know where the real money is. They are not coming here."

"Who asked you to butt in, Barb?" Star argued again. "Why don't you stick to the election?"

Betty Sue rapped the table with her hand.

"Stop beating a dead horse, Star, and shut up! Mandy, tell us what happens now."

"The concert is already sold out," Mandy said, reading something off her smart phone. "People from the surrounding states bought tickets because everyone wanted to hear this guy sing."

"So what now?" Molly echoed.

"We either cancel the concert and refund the tickets …"

"Can we really do that?" Jenny asked.

"The tickets were sold online so yeah, it's possible," Mandy nodded. "But it's not desirable. It gives the festival a bad name. And it will mean we won't reach any of our fund raising goals."

"Do we have any other option?" Star asked, finally looking beyond her perceived insult.

"We need to get someone else," Mandy said with a shrug. "Someone as famous as Ace Boulevard."

"Good luck with that," Heather muttered.

"What are the chances?" Jenny asked.

"Slim," Mandy said frankly. "It's short notice and most of these singers have full calendars."

"Looks like you have your work cut out then, young lady," Betty Sue said imperiously. "Start looking for a new artist for our concert."

Everyone pitched in with suggestions about what Mandy could do next. Barb settled down a bit after sampling some of Jenny's chocolates. The two women finally left, Barb spouting a steady set of instructions and Mandy bobbing her head up and down as she noted them all down.

"The nerve of that woman," Star fumed as soon as Barb was out of earshot. "She wants it all."

"Enough already, Star," Betty Sue said. "Think about

how to salvage the festival."

"What about some local band?" Jenny suggested. "I am sure they will be happy to get the exposure."

"They will," Heather said sarcastically, "but the people who bought the tickets won't. They are coming here to listen to a star, don't forget that."

Jason Stone hailed them from the boardwalk. He was hurrying along, pushing Emily's stroller.

"What's the matter, Jason?" Jenny cried when she noted his anxious expression.

"The police have arrested Ocean."

The women bombarded him with questions. Jason held up his hand.

"It's not entirely unexpected. I need to go bail him out. Can one of you look after Emily?"

"We need to prep for lunch," Star reminded Jenny.

"I can stay back and help watch the baby," Heather assured Jason.

Jason looked relieved. He promised to keep them posted and hurried off toward the police station.

"Ocean is that bearded fellow, right?" Betty Sue asked.

"He sure looks like a thug."

"Looks can be deceiving, Grandma," Heather said, dangling a set of keys before Emily. "Ocean is harmless."

"I say he's a thug," Betty Sue maintained.

"We don't have a lot of suspects," Jenny mused. "Ocean is the most obvious because he had a fight with Tyler."

"But Tyler was the one who pushed Ocean, remember?" Heather said. "We saw it with our own eyes."

They went back and forth over it for a while. Molly left to go back to her desk at the library and Betty Sue went back to the inn, pleading exhaustion. Heather took the baby back into the kitchen with Jenny and Star.

Jenny added fresh pesto to rotini pasta and tossed it with some finely diced olives and peppers. Jason arrived as the lunch rush was winding down.

"They let him go for now," he said, wringing a hand through his hair. "He is going to be their top suspect until he can prove he found that guitar on the beach."

"How is he taking it?" Jenny asked.

"Ask him yourself," Jason said. "I invited him here for lunch."

Ocean arrived and sat at a table on the deck. He ate the crab sandwich Jenny placed before him with relish.

"I suppose you are sorry you ever set foot in this town," Jenny said.

"We can't predict what's around the corner," Ocean said with a shrug. "It could have happened anywhere."

"What made you come to Pelican Cove?" Heather asked. "We are so off the beaten track."

"I was driving north from Georgia," Ocean told them. "Someone mentioned this scenic route via the Chesapeake. I thought I would check it out."

"There are plenty other towns along the Eastern Shore," Jenny prompted. "Why this one?"

"Why do we do anything?" Ocean drawled. "It just happened."

"Are troubadours always confrontational?" Heather asked. "Why didn't you leave when you found Tyler was already here?"

Ocean flashed a toothy smile.

"I fell in love with this town. It's become my muse. I

have written some really good songs since coming here."

"Isn't there a troubadour code?" Jason asked, drawn into the conversation. "I remember reading about it when I did some research for the case."

"It's more of a guideline," Ocean dismissed.

"That doesn't sound right," Jason said with a frown. "In fact, I distinctly remember that troubadours are like a close knit family. They look out for each other."

Heather was tapping some keys on her phone. She looked up and waited impatiently for Jason to stop talking.

"I just did some quick research," she burst out. "There's a nationwide group where you can register yourself. And there is an active database that lists who is playing in which town. A troubadour is supposed to check the status before he enters a town."

"We don't know if Tyler used that database," Jenny pointed out.

"But he did," Heather cried. "He is listed here as the official troubadour of Pelican Cove. That means no one else is allowed to play their music here."

Jenny put her hands on her hips and stared at Ocean

with raised eyebrows.

"I don't follow all that crap," he muttered. "Isn't there enough external influence in our life? The government dictates how we should live and how much tax we should pay. Now some unseen, unknown group is telling me where I can play my tunes?"

"So you knew you were barging in on Tyler's territory," Jenny summed up. "You just didn't care."

Ocean gave one of his habitual shrugs.

"Tyler didn't need the money. He had a big trust fund to fall back on. Unlike the rest of us."

"How do you know about Tyler's trust fund?" Jenny asked suddenly.

She thought hard, trying to remember. Had they discussed Tyler's background with Ocean?

Ocean struggled to his feet.

"I need to make a move. Already lost a few good hours of work today."

"You are hiding something," Heather said suddenly. "How did you know how rich Tyler was?"

"Can't say," he said, scratching his beard. "Must have heard it somewhere."

"I advise you to come clean, man," Jason said, speaking softly for Emily's sake.

She had fallen asleep after he fed and burped her.

"I am beginning to think you knew Tyler before coming here," Jenny said, taking a shot in the dark. "Admit it."

"No, I didn't," Ocean said.

"You are not telling us the whole truth," Jenny insisted. "How did you know Tyler came from a rich family?"

"Jenny will find out sooner or later," Heather warned. "She is good at ferreting out secrets."

"What happens when the police find out?" Jason asked Ocean. "You will be in more trouble than you are now. I need to know the truth if I am to defend you."

"Okay, okay," Ocean said, holding up his hands. "Give me a minute."

Ocean scratched his head and stared out at the waves for some time. He gave a deep sigh and started talking.

"I was paid to come here," he began.

"What?" Jenny and Heather echoed.

"I was playing my music in the Shenandoah valley when this rich dude came up to me. He placed a big bundle of cash in my hand."

"What did he want?" Jenny asked.

"Who was he?" Heather asked at the same time.

"This man said he was Tyler's uncle. Apparently, Tyler was supposed to run a fancy business. This dude didn't want him playing his guitar on the street."

"Did he ask you to harm Tyler?" Jenny narrowed her eyes.

"Not exactly," Ocean said with a shake of his head. "I was supposed to come here and make life hell for him."

"Did he say why?" Jason asked.

"Guess he wanted Tyler to give up this gig and go home."

"And you thought you could make him leave?"

"I thought it was a piece of cake," Ocean said. "I reckoned all I had to do was dog his steps. It was easy too. Turned out he had a really short temper. I thought he would pack up his guitar and hit the road."

"But he didn't leave, did he?" Jenny asked.

"No," Ocean nodded. "The kid had spunk."

"How far were you willing to go, Ocean?" Heather asked. "Did you sell your soul for a bit of money?"

Ocean looked disturbed.

"I just wanted the kid to go home. I didn't harm a hair on his head, honest."

Chapter 13

It was another busy day at the Boardwalk Café. Jenny had flipped dozens of blueberry pancakes, the special of the day. The parfaits were almost gone and she had run through four trays of banana nut muffins. Jenny was glad breakfast was almost over.

Heather came bouncing in, her face red with excitement. Jenny could tell she was bursting to share some news.

"Good Morning," Jenny greeted her with a smile. "What's got you all hot and bothered, my friend?"

"You'll never guess who just checked into the Bayview Inn," Heather beamed.

She grabbed Jenny by the arms and spun her around in a circle.

"Who?" Jenny asked, playing along.

"Bobby Joe Tucker!" Heather exclaimed.

Her eyes widened as she waited for Jenny to respond suitably.

"Should that name mean something to me?" Jenny asked drily.

"You have never heard of Bobby Joe Tucker?" Heather sucked in a breath as she stared at Jenny in disbelief. "Have you been living under a rock?"

"Apparently," Jenny laughed. "So who is this guy? Some old flame?"

"I wish," Heather sighed. "Bobby Joe is a top country singer. His latest single 'You are my everything' is top of the charts."

"I didn't know you were a country music fan."

"I'm not. I mean, not really. But I do know the latest hits."

"Is he from around here?" Jenny asked Heather.

"He's not," Heather confirmed. "What's he doing out here in the boonies?"

"Why don't you ask him?" Jenny suggested.

Heather couldn't get over her shock. She sat in a kitchen chair and went over different scenarios. She couldn't believe a big music star had checked into her inn.

"Shouldn't you be at the inn, making sure he's taken care of?" Jenny asked.

"He went out," Heather told her. "He's got this big RV. It's like a tour bus. He's in there working."

The Magnolias arrived for their daily coffee break. Heather repeated everything she had told Jenny.

"I don't like the look of him," Betty Sue said suspiciously. "He better not steal our towels."

"Come on Grandma!" Heather said, scandalized. "He sold a million records just last month. He doesn't care for our towels."

"You never know," Betty Sue said staunchly. "He's not an islander after all."

Heather looked irritated.

"Most of the people who come to our inn aren't," she told Betty Sue.

"And they steal stuff," Betty Sue said triumphantly. "Don't they? Didn't we just replace a dozen towels and five bath robes?"

Heather opened her mouth to object. Jenny stepped in to calm them down.

"Let it go, you two. How long is this illustrious guest staying in town?"

Heather's face lit up again.

"He's paid a big advance. He should be here for a couple of weeks at least. Why?"

"Just a thought," Jenny said. "Do you think he will sing at our fall festival?"

Jenny's question created an uproar. Everyone started talking at once. Star wanted to go and talk to him at once.

"Isn't the Pelican Cove fall fest too low key for this guy?" Molly provided a practical opinion.

"Fall festival is a month away," Betty Sue said. "Surely he won't stay with us that long."

"How much will he charge?" Jenny asked. "Can we afford to hire him?"

"All of these are good questions," Heather said. "We need to come up with a solid plan before we approach him. I think we need Mandy's help."

"What does she know that we don't?" Star asked.

She was still holding a grudge against Mandy.

"Mandy's good at her job," Jenny reasoned. "She is used to dealing with celebrities. She will know how to approach this Bobby Joe."

"What's this country music star doing in Pelican Cove?" Molly asked.

"I think he needs a break. This is the best place for someone who wants to fly below the radar."

"I'm tired of talking about this boy," Betty Sue said, pulling out her knitting from a tote bag. "And I'm hungry."

Jenny took the hint and went in to get some fresh muffins.

"When are we going to the city, Jenny?" Heather asked. "I thought you wanted to leave early."

Jenny had received another call from Mr. Jones in Richmond. He wanted to meet her.

"You can leave now," Star told them. "Lunch is caprese sandwiches. I can easily make them."

Jenny made sure her aunt had everything she needed. She packed some lunch for herself and Heather and they set off for Richmond. It was a good two hour drive.

The butler ushered them into the parlor. Mr. Jones was waiting for them this time. He looked pale and had a racking cough.

"Are you sick, Mr. Jones?" Jenny asked with concern.

"Don't worry, gel," he croaked. "I'm not dying anytime soon."

Jenny couldn't figure out if he was irritated or being humorous. Mr. Jones asked about the progress Jenny had made.

"I seem to have hit a wall," Jenny admitted.

She told the old man about the two suspects.

"But you don't think much about them, eh?" the old man asked shrewdly.

"I do believe they are both innocent," Jenny admitted. "But that leaves us with no suspects."

The old man cleared his throat.

"What do you think of my son?" he asked bluntly.

Jenny hesitated.

"I haven't really met him, Mr. Jones. What possible motive could he have to harm Tyler?"

The old man was quiet. Jenny gave him some time and then spoke up tentatively.

"How is he situated financially?"

"My son is a very wealthy man," Mr. Jones said. "So is

my grandson."

"And he gets even more money now that Tyler is gone?"

"He does," the old man nodded. "My son believed he was entitled to that money."

Jenny sensed there was more to the story. She sat back in her chair and waited for Mr. Jones to continue.

"Tyler …" the old man began. "Tyler was the apple of my eye."

His rheumy eyes filled up as he spoke about his grandson.

"He was a good person, a better person than my son."

Heather nudged Jenny and pulled a face. Was the old man just rambling or did his talk have a purpose? Jenny gave Heather a stare, silently warning her to be quiet.

"I loved Tyler very much," the old man continued. "That didn't sit too well with my son."

He looked up at Jenny and she sensed he was about to say something important.

"You see, Ms. King. Tyler was adopted."

Jenny let out a gasp. She hadn't seen that coming.

"I still remember the day his parents brought him home," the old man reminisced. "He was barely a month old. He was a Jones from that moment on."

"Was he related to you?" Jenny asked.

She wondered if Tyler had been adopted from a poor relative.

"No idea where he came from," Mr. Jones said. "It was a closed adoption. My son, Tyler's uncle, was against it at the time."

"How did he treat Tyler?"

"He rallied around," the old man told them. "Tyler was such a sweet kid. He looked up to his uncle, especially after his parents died."

"What changed?" Jenny asked.

"It was the music," Mr. Jones said with a sigh. "Tyler was supposed to start learning the business. But he seemed more interested in writing songs. My son thought it was a waste of time."

"Tyler could have written his music in his spare time," Jenny mused. "Surely he was brought up with certain expectations?"

"He was," the old man agreed. "Tyler was groomed to be at the helm of a bunch of companies."

The old man's gaze hardened.

"Tyler was doing fine until he found out he was adopted."

"You had never told him?"

"His parents might have at some point. But he was just a child when they died. I guess it was my job to tell him when he grew up. But I decided not to. Still don't know how he found out."

Jenny thought it was kind of obvious but she didn't say anything.

"He took it hard?" Jenny guessed.

The old man's voice shook as he replied to Jenny.

"He started behaving erratically. He stopped going in to work. I think he must have latched on to this troubadour business around that time."

"Your son didn't like that, I guess?"

"They had a big fight," the old man said. "My son warned Tyler to clean up his act."

Jenny leaned forward and patted the old man's knee.

"What are you afraid of, Mr. Jones?"

"He wouldn't … he wouldn't do something drastic, would he? He can't be that heartless."

"I don't think so," Jenny soothed.

She told him what she had learned from Ocean. It seemed like Tyler's uncle just wanted him to come back home.

"That does seem more plausible," Mr. Jones said, sounding relieved. "Sounds like something he would do. Throw money at a problem and expect it to go away."

Jenny wasn't taking any chances. She asked Mr. Jones if she could look around a bit. She pointed her phone toward some photos on the mantel and started clicking pictures. She did the same thing with a couple of cars parked outside.

"What are you doing, Jenny?" Heather whispered. "I thought you agreed the uncle was innocent."

"I'm just making sure," Jenny said softly. "I will explain later."

Mr. Jones was talking to his son when they went back in. He gave Jenny and Heather a withering look.

"Are you here to poison the old man against me?"

Jenny decided to beard the lion in his den.

"You have made it clear you didn't like Tyler."

"I didn't like how he was throwing away his life. He was going to be twenty five soon. He needed to get his act together and start acting responsibly."

"That's all?"

"Believe it or not, yes," the man thundered. "If you think otherwise, prove it."

"I am working on that," Jenny said boldly.

"You are on the wrong track," he said, his voice full of scorn. "Obviously, you have nothing better to do. Tell me, how much is my father paying you? I will pay you triple to stop nosing around."

"You fool!" Old Mr. Jones roared. "Everything can't be measured in money. Ms. King has very kindly agreed to help us. She isn't taking a cent from me."

"Don't be naïve, Dad. Someone else must be paying her. Some trashy tabloid, probably."

Jenny tried to curb the anger she felt. She decided to exit gracefully. She said goodbye to Mr. Jones and promised to stay in touch. She walked out with

Heather following close behind.

"That was intense," Heather gushed as Jenny drove her car out of the massive iron gates. "Were you provoking him on purpose?"

Jenny cracked a smile and shrugged.

"Where to?" she asked Heather.

"You still haven't chosen your wedding dress," Heather reminded her dourly. "Why don't we check out a few bridal stores while we are here? I have a list with me."

"Molly's not with us again," Jenny reminded her.

"I know," Heather grimaced. "But do you want to waste this opportunity?"

"I still think we should look closer to home," Jenny said. "Coming to Richmond for fittings sounds like a chore."

"Why don't you choose something first?" Heather sighed. "We can figure out the rest later."

"What about your dress?" Jenny asked. "You can choose any style you want. No hideous bridesmaid dresses at my wedding."

"We already thought about it," Heather smirked. "We are going with fall colors. We are all wearing shades of yellow, orange or russet."

"That sounds beautiful," Jenny said, her eyes filling up.

"Don't you get maudlin now, Jenny King!" Heather warned. "We are just getting started on our wedding chores."

Chapter 14

The town square was jammed with people. Tourists mingled with locals, looking on with interest as volunteers set up a makeshift stage. It was the day of the debate. Peter Wilson had challenged Barb Norton for the first public debate before the election and she had no choice but to accept.

Supporters on both sides had plastered the town with flyers advertising the event. Everyone was invited. No one would have dreamed of missing it.

People sat on camp chairs with coolers by their side, ready to enjoy a good show. Some people had brought picnic hampers and reclined on blankets. Kids scurried about, chasing each other and screaming their heads off.

Jenny had her own agenda for the debate.

The Magnolias had set up their chairs in two semi-circles. Betty Sue and Star sat at either end. Heather and Jenny sat in between. Molly sat in the second row with Chris. The other two spots were reserved for Jason and Adam. Adam was on duty, keeping the crowd in check. Heather had made gallons of popcorn. Jenny had brought her latest batch of truffles and Molly had brought brownies. They were all set to listen to arguments from both sides. Star was confident Barb would win. Betty Sue was the only one who supported Peter Wilson.

A lot of locals stopped by them to greet the ladies. Jenny had her phone out. She flipped through the screen and showed them the photos she had taken at the Jones residence.

"Do any of these people look familiar?" she asked. "What about these cars?"

Most people barely glanced at the screen before shaking their heads. Others peered at the screen ghoulishly and reluctantly gave it back.

"You really think you can catch a murderer that way?" Star asked skeptically.

"I just want to find out if one of them came to town."

"What if they did?" Molly asked. "That doesn't prove anything."

Jenny didn't have an answer for that. She admitted to herself that she was just grasping at straws.

Captain Charlie came and sat with the women. Betty Sue started talking to the old salt.

"Do you agree we don't need more tourists in town?"

Captain Charlie ran fishing tours. His business depended on the tourists.

"I wouldn't say that exactly," he said, stroking his beard. "This town as good as runs on tourists, you know."

"But what about all the mess they create?" Betty Sue cried. "Look around you. The town's never been this dirty."

"We need more people on cleaning duty then," Captain Charlie said with a shrug.

He looked at Jenny for support. Jenny thrust her phone in his face.

"Can you take a look at this?" she asked. "Anyone look familiar?"

Captain Charlie scrolled through all the photos patiently before shaking his head.

"You better eat some of this popcorn, Jenny," Heather said, her fingers smeared with butter. "It's almost gone."

"She's right," Chris said, licking his fingers.

Jenny could barely think of food.

She started working the crowd, showing the photos to random people, urging people to look carefully as her frustration rose.

Someone grabbed her arm and pulled her aside. She whirled around to complain and found herself staring into a familiar pair of blue eyes.

"Adam!" she breathed. "It's you."

She put her arms around his neck and leaned in for a kiss. Adam jerked back and flung her hands away.

"Not here, Jenny. I am working."

Jenny's face fell as she tried to hide her disappointment.

"We saved a seat for you," she told him. "You can't miss us. Almost everyone's there except Jason and Emily. But they will be along soon."

"What do you think you are doing, Jenny?" Adam asked angrily. "People are beginning to complain."

"I have some pictures of Tyler's family," she began to explain. "I just want to know if anyone saw them in town."

"I don't care," Adam snapped. "I am warning you, Jenny. Stop this nonsense right now."

"Nonsense?" Jenny asked, placing her hands on her hips.

"I don't have time to argue with you," Adam said, starting to walk away. "Stop harassing people or I will have to take you in."

"You can't do that," Jenny challenged.

"I can and I will," Adam said, sounding exasperated. "Don't test my patience, Jenny. I won't be able to do you any favors. You are being a nuisance."

Adam turned his back on her and walked away. Jenny's eyes filled up as she stared at him. Why couldn't he cut her some slack? Then she remembered how Adam preferred to keep his professional life separate from his private one. She forced herself to admire his integrity.

"You look like someone slapped you," Star commented as soon as she spotted Jenny.

"Adam must have said something," Heather piped up. "He can be so nasty."

Jason had arrived with Emily. She sat in her stroller, dressed in a cheery yellow frock and stared around her with interest. Jason's nose twitched in annoyance as he looked at Jenny.

"What is it? What grave crime are you supposed to

have committed this time?"

"Forget it," Jenny said feebly. "It's nothing."

"Why don't you eat something?" Molly coaxed. "Jason brought pizza."

Jenny forced herself to eat a slice and immediately felt better.

Eddie Cotton from the pub joined them. He sat with Betty Sue and Star, arguing about whether Pelican Cove needed tourists or not.

"I thought you would be at the pub," Star said.

"Most of the people are here," he said. "I thought I would stretch my legs. I wanted to put up a beer stand but Barb said no."

Jenny flipped through her phone again, moodily staring at her pictures.

"What's that you have there, Jenny?" Eddie asked.

Jenny handed over her phone to him.

Eddie scrolled through the photos half heartedly, continuing an impassioned dialog with Betty Sue and Star. A few moments later, he let out a sudden exclamation.

"I know him," he said, jabbing his finger at the screen. "I bet he has been to the Rusty Anchor a couple of times."

Jenny realized he was pointing at a picture of Billy Jones, Tyler's cousin.

"Tell me more," she pressed. "Was he alone? Was he talking to someone?"

"I don't remember that much," Eddie said, handing the phone back to her. "At least not now. Maybe it will come to me."

"Please try to remember," Jenny urged him. "This may be important."

"Okay, missy," Eddie nodded. "Give me some time."

The loudspeaker crackled as Mandy came on stage and began testing the microphone. Both the candidates climbed up on stage and greeted the crowd. A wild cry went up. Both Peter Wilson and Barb Norton had worked hard for the debate. Jenny forgot everything else as she listened to them in rapt attention. Questions flew from the crowd and both candidates handled them deftly. The debate ended in a tie.

"That went better than I expected," Star said as Jenny drove them home. "I never expected Peter would speak so well. Not with his background."

"He did seem prepared," Jenny admitted grudgingly. "And sounds like he is passionate about the cause too."

"He can't really be against tourism though, can he?" Star quizzed. "He is a business owner too."

"Most of his customers are locals," Jenny explained. "How many tourists are going to get an oil change at his garage?"

Back home, Star set up her easel in the garden. Jenny decided to take a nap.

Two hours later, Jenny woke up refreshed. She fired off a text to Adam and confirmed that he was coming for dinner. She decided to make her special paella.

"You can win any man's heart with your cooking, Jenny," Star offered as she chopped vegetables. "But not Adam's. He's a tough one."

"I already have his heart," Jenny said smugly.

"Doesn't look like it," Star muttered.

She had never hidden the fact that she wasn't a big fan of Adam. Jenny worried about their living situation after she got married. She had invited her aunt to make her home with her at Seaview. But would Adam and Star get along?

Adam arrived with a bottle of Jenny's favorite wine and a bunch of daisies. Jenny melted as soon as she saw the look on his face.

Star pleaded exhaustion and decided to eat in her room.

Jenny and Adam sat out on the patio, sipping wine and watching the sun creep closer to the horizon. The sky was aflame in shades of orange interspersed with pink and purple. The water glistened in the rays of the setting sun.

"Did your hunting expedition yield anything?" Adam asked.

Jenny felt Adam was taunting her. She decided to say nothing about Eddie.

"You were right, Adam. I shouldn't have bothered those people."

"You have been an invaluable help to the police many times, Jenny. I will be the first one to admit that. But I think you are stumbling in the dark this time."

"There does seem to be a dearth of suspects," Jenny said glumly.

"I say we have the right suspect," Adam argued. "My money is still on that Ocean chap."

"You don't have any concrete evidence," Jenny reminded him.

"I still believe he is guilty," Adam insisted. "I won't rest until I put him away."

"What about motive?" Jenny questioned. "Ocean is an easygoing chap. What could he possibly have against Tyler?"

"He was jealous," Adam said. "He just wanted to eliminate the competition. Men have been killed for less."

"Peter Wilson should be top on your list in that case," Jenny pointed out. "He was spitting mad at Tyler. He even threatened him."

"I don't think Peter did it."

"You are willing to ignore his past record?" Jenny wondered. "Why, Adam?"

"Peter Wilson has been an exemplary citizen of this town for the past twenty five years. This Ocean chap is an outsider."

"Is that all?"

"Give me some credit," Adam sighed. "We ran a background check on Ocean. His movements are highly suspicious. He has been in regions where there were break-ins and robberies. One of the towns he was in had a fire just the night before he left town."

"You are saying he committed all those crimes?" Jenny asked with contempt. "You are just determined to pin something on him."

"I have my reasons, Jenny."

Ocean's serene face swam before Jenny's eyes. She couldn't believe Adam wanted to pin a litany of crimes on him.

"I think you are on a witch hunt."

"I'm just doing my job, Jenny," Adam said grimly.

Jenny forced herself to change the subject. She didn't want to end the evening on a sour note.

"How are the girls? Nicky said they should all be here in a couple of weeks."

Adam's girls were doing a summer internship in the city. So was Jenny's son Nick. Much to their relief, Jenny and Adam's kids were good friends. They were looking forward to spending a few days in Pelican Cove before going back to college in the fall.

Adam relaxed at the mention of his girls.

"Have you asked them yet?"

"I want to talk to them in person," Jenny told him. "I hope they will say yes."

"Of course they will say yes. It's all they have been talking about all summer."

Adam's phone trilled just then, making him frown. He answered gruffly and his mouth hung open as he listened to the voice at the other end.

Jenny leaned forward, waiting for Adam to speak. Adam looked very upset as he stared at Jenny.

"You were right about Ocean."

Chapter 15

The Magnolias chatted at the top of their voices, guzzling coffee and commenting on the tourists that lined the beach. Jenny felt she was the only one affected by Ocean's death. Murder, she corrected herself.

They had found Ocean's body on a deserted beach. Based on initial examination, the police were thinking he had walked into the sea and drowned. He had luckily been washed ashore. Jenny wasn't sure she believed that.

She felt Heather staring at her and snapped to attention.

"Did you say anything, Heather?"

Heather rolled her eyes.

"I have been asking you the same question three times. Have you heard 'You are my everything'?"

"Is that supposed to mean something to me?"

"It's only the name of Bobby Joe's hit single," Heather gushed. "It hit the top spot last night."

"Oh," Jenny muttered. "I don't listen to country music."

"You have to give it a chance," Heather insisted. "Especially since Bobby Joe is staying right here with us."

"That does it," Star said. "He's not going to sing for us now. He's too famous."

"You haven't even asked him yet!" Heather cried. "He has a big fan base here. Why would he refuse?"

"Let's go ask him now," Betty Sue said, struggling to her feet.

"Yes, let's," Star said, scrambling up. "I want to get this done before that maniac Barb Norton thinks about it."

"Too late," Molly said, nodding at the boardwalk.

Barb Norton and Mandy were walking toward the café.

"Yoohooo!" Barb called out her usual greeting. "Going somewhere?"

"No time to waste, Barb," Star quipped. "We are on an important mission."

"Never mind, then. I thought you would want to go with us. Mandy and I are going to invite Bobby Joe

Tucker to play at the fall festival."

"That's where we are going," Betty Sue objected. "No need to waste your time, Barb. Go talk to your voters."

"The voters can wait," Barb said lightly. "This is more important."

Then she giggled like a school girl.

"Mandy says this boy is quite the looker. I can't wait to see him."

"Have you ever heard him sing?" Heather asked skeptically. "Do you even know what kind of music he plays?"

"Of course I do," Barb said in a huff. "It's country with a pop influence. Mandy played his hit single for me. I have been humming it all morning."

"That's more than I can say for my grandma," Heather said grudgingly.

"Who cares if we know his music or not?" Betty Sue spat. "We want to go and talk to him. He is living in my house so there is no doubt I am going."

"Let's all go," Mandy said, trying to placate the older women. "We will look like a delegation and he will feel more welcome."

Betty Sue and Star joined Barb and Mandy, talking eagerly about how to approach him.

"This is going to be the best fall festival yet," Heather sighed dramatically. "Just imagine! Bobby Joe Tucker playing in tiny old Pelican Cove!"

"He hasn't said yes yet," Jenny pointed out. "I imagine he will charge a pretty penny."

"I didn't think of that," Heather admitted. "I thought he would just sing for the sake of his fans."

"That's not how these stars function," Molly said practically. "They have to make a living too, I guess. What's he doing in Pelican Cove though?"

"Living off the grid," Heather parroted. "That's what he calls it."

"I'm going to the Rusty Anchor this evening," Jenny told them. "I need to talk to Eddie Cotton. You girls coming?"

Heather and Molly promised to meet Jenny later at the pub.

Jenny got busy prepping for lunch. She made a pot full of watermelon gazpacho. The cold Spanish style soup was a summer favorite. Jenny had chucked in some leftover watermelon in it once and it had been a huge hit.

Star came back just in time to help her serve some lunch. She wasn't looking too happy.

"What's the matter? Didn't you get to meet that singer guy?"

"I met him alright," Star grumbled. "But he's beyond our reach. There's no way we can afford to hire him."

"Didn't you ask him to give us a discount?" Jenny asked later when they sat down for their own lunch.

Star bit into her crab salad sandwich and shook her head.

"He's taking a big chunk off his usual rate, apparently. He said he wants to do something for the people of Pelican Cove. But it's still more than our budget."

"Guess we will have to hire some other band," Jenny said. Her eyes flickered with emotion. "Ocean would have done it for free."

Star helped Jenny clear up and prep for the next day. Jenny drove home with her. She had a couple of hours before she had to be at the pub. She decided to relax in her garden until then. Jenny changed into a pair of shorts and a bikini top and settled into a cabana she had installed in her garden. Putting her arms below her head, she stared out at the ocean. She started to get hot after some time and walked into the water for a quick dip. She almost forgot she needed to go out again.

The Rusty Anchor was packed when she got there. Every table was taken and there was barely a space open to stand at the bar. Eddie Cotton pointed at a battered door. She had never noticed it before.

"It's a little hidey hole for my special people," he told her. "The pub gets too crowded in the season."

Jenny entered a small, darkened room, barely lit by an ancient bronze chandelier. Heather and Molly were seated at a table under it. They both had a glass of wine before them.

"I'll come back and check on you soon," Eddie promised.

Jenny chatted with the girls half-heartedly, waiting for Eddie to come back. He arrived with a platter of chicken wings Heather had ordered earlier.

"Do you remember the photos I was showing you?" Jenny asked him. "You said one of them looked familiar. What can you tell me about him?"

"You mean that chubby kid with a paunch? He came here a lot a few weeks ago."

"Do you remember who he talked to?"

"Was a bit of a weirdo, if you ask me. Picked a few fights over nothin'. Had to warn him to lighten up."

"Is that all?" Jenny pressed.

Eddie's face cleared as he remembered something.

"Now that you mention it – I saw him talking to that troubadour a couple of times."

"Did you hear what they were talking about?"

Eddie hesitated.

"I wasn't paying attention. I can't be too sure but I think they were arguing about something."

Jenny wondered why Tyler's cousin had come all the way to Pelican Cove to pick a fight with him.

"Do you know what Tyler did after he left the pub every night?"

"Drove home to Richmond," Eddie said.

"Are you sure?" Jenny asked.

"100%. Talked about what a pain it was driving a couple of hours each way."

Jenny was stumped. If Tyler had gone home every day, Billy could have easily met him at home. What had he been up to? Had Tyler been in on it?

"Gotta go," Eddie said before rushing to take care of someone else.

"What's this, Jenny?" Heather pouted. "I thought we were having a girls' night."

Jenny devoted herself to her girlfriends after that. Heather was lamenting the lack of eligible men in Pelican Cove.

"Adam and Chris were the only handsome hunks and you both grabbed them," Heather said, her tongue loose after her second glass of wine.

"What about Jason?" Jenny asked. "He is as eligible as they come."

"Ewww …" Heather cried. "Jason is like a brother to me."

"What about Ethan?" Molly asked, referring to Adam's brother. "Didn't he just break up with his girl?"

Ethan Hopkins was a divorcee with no kids. He had been dating someone for the past few years. They had recently had a very public breakup when the girl left him for someone living in the city.

"Ethan's still licking his wounds," Heather clucked. "And I have a feeling those two aren't done yet. City life is not for everyone."

"He can still be your date for the wedding," Jenny offered. "He is the best man and you are my maid of honor."

"I don't know, Jenny," Heather slurred. "Those Hopkins boys are trouble."

"Do you have any other date for Jenny's wedding?" Molly asked.

"Why can't I go alone?" Heather challenged. "I am a modern independent woman. I don't need a man to hold my hand."

"Bravo!" Jenny clapped her hands. "That's the kind of spirit I like."

"Speaking of the wedding," Molly said. "We still need to talk about flowers. Do you have a city florist in mind?"

"We don't need a florist, Molly," Jenny deadpanned. "I want flowers from my garden. My very own roses and gardenias. I can't imagine any other bouquet for the wedding."

"If you insist," Molly said. "I guess that's one more

item we can check off the list."

"Please tell me you are not baking your own cake," Heather said drily.

"I want to," Jenny confessed. "But I am not sure if I will have the time."

"I know a very good bakery in Virginia Beach," Molly told them. "Please order your cake from them, Jenny. They are really good."

"You are skimping on almost everything," Heather pointed out. "Barbecue instead of caterers, flowers from your own garden … splurge on the cake. Order a lavish four tiered thing. You deserve it."

"I will set up an appointment for us," Molly said before Jenny could object. "We need to go cake tasting."

Jenny and the girls lingered at the pub for a couple of hours. Jenny was ready to call it a night by the time she got home. A bank of clouds had crept up the horizon, shadowing the moon. She spotted a familiar figure on the beach as she parked her car. A large furry body came bounding up as soon as she stepped down. Jenny hugged the yellow Labrador and scratched him below the ears.

"Tank! I missed you!"

Tank had been with Adam through thick and thin. Jenny was besotted with him. He had been staying with Adam's brother for the past few weeks, keeping him company while he mooned over his lost love. Jenny had missed spending time with him.

Adam walked up to Jenny. He was using his cane again. Jenny wanted to ask if his leg was hurting badly but she forced herself to stay quiet.

"Looks like you had a wild time."

His tone was clipped and Jenny decided he was definitely in pain. She wondered if he would give in and take a pain pill.

"It was just Heather and Molly," she said with a shrug. "You coming in?"

Adam shook his head.

"Tank and I need to get back. I have to get up early. I am going to the city."

"Is everything alright?" Jenny asked, picking up on the tension.

Was Adam jealous of the time she had spent with the girls? They would need to have a talk about it again. She wasn't ready to be shackled down in any way just because she was getting married to him.

Adam swallowed and sighed deeply.

"It's official. Ocean was murdered. The news has already leaked out. I thought I would tell you myself."

"I knew it!" Jenny crowed. "So he didn't just drown?"

Adam shook his head.

"According to the autopsy report, Ocean was strangled."

Chapter 16

Jenny wasn't having a good day. She had barely slept, thoughts of Ocean's last moments keeping her awake. When she did manage to fall asleep toward dawn, she had nightmares. She woke up drenched in sweat, shaking in fear at some unknown assailant who had been about to choke her.

She had overslept after that and hadn't reached the café until 6 AM. That meant breakfast had been late. She had to send Captain Charlie away without his muffin.

Star had been on the phone for twenty minutes. Jenny felt her irritation rise. She tried to tune out the one sided conversation and focused on making her stuffed French Toast. Loaded with fresh strawberries, it was a summer favorite at the Boardwalk Café.

Star gave a whoop and finally hung up.

"Guess what?" she crowed, clapping her hands.

"Why don't you just tell me?" Jenny asked crankily.

"Someone woke up on the wrong side of bed today," Star said with a smile.

"Star ..." Jenny groaned.

"Okay, okay. You will never believe what just happened. The town has agreed to pay that Bobby Joe person. We have one hot concert coming up, Jenny. Right here too, in Pelican Cove."

"I thought we couldn't afford him?" Jenny quizzed.

"You know how Barb is when she wants something. She called a meeting of the town council. They just voted to cough up the money."

"Where is this money coming from?" Jenny asked, sprinkling powdered sugar over a plate of toast.

"From the reserves," Star explained. "This is historic, Jenny. The town has never dipped in the reserves. The reserves are sacred."

"What's so special about this guy then?" Jenny asked with a grimace.

"His song is number one in the country, Jenny. And he is willing to perform it live for the first time. Right here on our beach."

"He better be worth it," Jenny muttered.

"Aren't you going to Richmond today?" Star asked.

Jenny nodded.

"I was planning to go after lunch. We are going to be super busy, judging by the breakfast crowd."

Jenny's prediction proved to be right. She made dozens of sandwiches and salads while Star ladled endless bowls of seafood chowder. Both women were exhausted.

Jenny put her feet up on a chair as she wolfed down her own sandwich.

"Look at those cracked heels," Star clucked as she stared at Jenny's feet. "How many times should I tell you, Jenny. You are going to be a bride. You need to take better care of yourself."

"Maybe we should have a spa night," Jenny said grudgingly.

"I have a better idea," Star said. "Let's all go to that day spa in Cape Charles. We need to do a test run before your wedding anyway. We can book all your bridal treatments there if you like the place."

"Sounds pricey." Jenny made a face.

"It's your wedding," Star said. "You can afford to spend a bit."

"Whatever you say, Aunt," Jenny sighed. "I wonder what's keeping Heather."

"I'm right here," Heather said, sweeping in.

She was grinning from ear to ear.

"Bobby Joe came out of his room to get coffee. I said hello to him and he said hello back."

"Shouldn't he?" Jenny asked.

"Oh Jenny! You don't get it. Bobby Joe Tucker spoke to me! It was my big fan girl moment."

"You sound as mad as the rest of the town," Jenny said. "They are going to shell out the big bucks needed for his gig."

"I know!" Heather beamed. "We are going to be famous. People are already asking each other where this island is where Bobby Joe Tucker is hiding out at."

"Shouldn't you get going?" Star reminded them.

Jenny took off her apron and freshened up a bit. She asked Heather to drive, pleading exhaustion.

Heather kept up a monologue all the way to Richmond. Jenny napped fitfully, barely hearing anything Heather said. Two hours later, Heather wove her way through downtown traffic to the more upscale River Road area.

The Jones residence loomed over them, reminding

Jenny once again of Tyler's exclusive background. The butler greeted them with a smile.

"Mr. Jones will be happy to see you."

"Actually, we were hoping to talk to Tyler's cousin."

"Master Billy is a bit indisposed," the butler said, clearing his throat.

"This could be important," Jenny told him.

"I will see what I can do," the butler promised.

Jenny had remembered to bring a big box of her truffles for Mr. Jones. She hoped he liked chocolates.

Billy Jones waddled in fifteen minutes later, looking like he had just got out of bed. He looked freshly showered but his eyes were bloodshot and his mouth was set in a frown.

"What do you want from me?" he grumbled.

"We need your help," Jenny began. "I hope you don't mind answering a few questions."

Billy spotted the box of chocolates and tore it open. He popped a couple of truffles in his mouth and chewed noisily.

"This is good stuff," Billy spoke, his teeth smeared

with chocolate. "I don't suppose you get these in that hick town of yours?"

"Jenny made them herself," Heather said curtly.

"You don't like Pelican Cove?" Jenny asked Billy.

"Never been there," he drawled. "Tyler was crazy about that place though."

"We know you visited the Rusty Anchor a few times," Jenny said to him. "The bartender recognized you."

"Why would you lie about going to Pelican Cove?" Heather asked.

"I don't want my Dad to find out," Billy said, looking over his shoulder.

"We won't tell him anything," Jenny promised. "Will you talk to us?"

Billy pulled his shirt down over his ample belly and frowned. He gave them a brief nod as his mouth settled into a pout.

"Okay."

"What were you doing in Pelican Cove?" Jenny asked a straightforward question.

"Tyler and I grew up together, in this house," Billy told

them. "I am a lot older than him but we were buddies while growing up. Very few kids in class were as rich as us. We got kind of isolated."

Jenny and Heather got caught up in Billy's story.

"What I'm saying is, I was used to looking out for Tyler. He told me everything he did. He wanted to write music for the rest of his life. My dad didn't want that, of course. When Tyler found this little island in the middle of nowhere, he was excited. He said they would let him play his songs all day long. He was happy."

"Based on what we learned, your father found out about it," Jenny told him.

"That was my fault," Billy admitted. "I let it slip. I went there to warn Tyler about it."

"What were you afraid of?"

"My father has a lot of influence," Billy said. "He would have made sure Tyler packed up his guitar and came home. I just wanted to give Tyler a heads up. We did that for each other all the time."

"Was Tyler going to come home with you?"

Billy shook his head.

"He was really fired up this time. He said people loved his music. He asked me to book a recording studio here in town. He was going to go all out with his song."

"Eddie at the pub told us that Tyler drove home every night?" Jenny asked.

"That's right," Billy laughed. "He tried roughing it out for a couple of nights. Get the authentic experience. But he wasn't cut out for it. Said he could bear standing in the sun all day but he needed his feather bed at night and fresh squeezed orange juice in the morning."

"So why did you go to the Rusty Anchor to talk to him?" Jenny asked. "You could have talked to him right here?"

"I wanted to see what the fuss was about."

"Surely you had heard him sing before?" Heather asked.

Billy's manner changed abruptly.

"I don't have to explain myself to you."

"Did you need a change of scene?" Jenny asked diplomatically.

"Hey, it's summer. And there's not much to do here.

So I wanted to get some beach action. So what?"

"So you took a road trip with Tyler and worked on your tan," Jenny said with a smile.

"Nothing of that sort," Billy said, shaking his head. "I drove there in my own car and came back on my own. Tyler didn't want to let on he knew me."

"Do you drive that Ferrari in the garage?" Jenny asked impishly.

"Sometimes," Billy said noncommittally. "Sometimes I take the Porsche."

"What did Tyler drive?" Jenny asked.

"He wanted to look poor," Billy said, fighting off a yawn. "He borrowed our housekeeper's ancient Toyota. Took him hours to get there in that trap."

"You and Tyler were brothers, right?" Jenny asked. "Did you fight like brothers too?"

"Who said we had a fight?" Billy asked sullenly.

"You were seen arguing with Tyler at the pub," Jenny said softly. "What was that about?"

"It was between us," Billy said. "Family stuff."

"Tyler's gone," Jenny reminded him. "And I am trying

to find out who had it in for him. This is not the time to withhold information."

Billy looked around before leaning forward. His voice had dropped to a whisper.

"It was that girl."

"What girl?"

No one had mentioned a girl in connection with Tyler until now.

"Must be some local chick," Billy said with a frown. "Tyler was crazy about her."

"What was the problem?"

"She was a gold digger," Billy said flatly. "They all are. She just wanted Tyler's money."

"How can you be so sure?" Heather asked. "And wait a minute, how did she know Tyler had money?"

"Tyler let it slip that he was coming into money very soon. That's when she started acting smitten."

"Was she hoping to marry Tyler?" Jenny asked.

"I don't know," Billy said. "My guess is she was going to blackmail Tyler. His whole street singer cred was based on him being poor."

"What were you arguing about exactly?"

"He wanted to bring her here to meet the old man. Not a good idea!"

Jenny couldn't determine whether Billy was right about the girl.

"Do you know her name?" Jenny asked. "Did you meet her yourself?"

Billy shook his head.

"Tyler was very protective about her."

Jenny looked up at the sound of shuffling feet. A voice could be heard grumbling outside. Mr. Jones came in a few moments later, followed by the butler.

"Jenny King!" he exclaimed. "Were we supposed to meet today?"

He glared at the old retainer.

"Why didn't anyone tell me she was here?"

Jenny picked up the open box of truffles.

"Do you like chocolates? I brought these for you."

The old man stared suspiciously at the box she held out. His hand shook as it hovered over the box. He finally made a choice and picked one up. He popped it in his mouth tentatively and a smile lit up his face.

"Who makes these?" he asked. "I want to invest in this company."

"Jenny made these herself," Heather supplied. "You can say they are home made."

"You can make a fortune with these," Mr. Jones told Jenny. "They are that good. Why don't you make an appointment with my office? I will ask my assistant to make a project plan. We can produce this on a large scale and sell them all over the country."

"Thank you Mr. Jones," Jenny blushed. "But I am not here to sell the truffles."

The old man's face fell as he snapped back to reality.

"Have you made any progress, Jenny?" he asked with a quaver. "Do you know who killed my boy?"

Chapter 17

Back home, Jenny got ready for dinner but her heart wasn't in it. It had been a while since she had spent any quality time with Adam. So she should have been excited about their date. But her mind kept drifting back to the troubadours and the fate that had befallen them.

Her search for Tyler's killer hadn't led to any new suspects. Now Ocean had met a similar fate. Jenny wondered if their profession had anything to do with the tragedy. Was there some kind of music hater out there who had a silent vendetta against singers? The idea seemed ridiculous even as she half heartedly considered it.

Adam would be no help in discovering anything about Ocean. Jenny was sure he would fly off the handle if she mentioned either crime during dinner. She reminded herself to stay away from the topic.

Adam had reservations at their favorite restaurant a couple of towns away. His eyes darkened as he gazed at Jenny over a plate of Beef Bourguignon.

"Just a few more days to go, Jenny," he said softly. "I can't wait."

"Me neither," Jenny said honestly.

Apart from the unsolved issue about their living arrangements, Jenny was looking forward to wedded bliss with Adam.

"How is the wedding planning coming along?" Adam asked. "Have you thrown any tantrums yet?"

"Not much scope for that," Jenny said, spearing a piece of thyme and lemon scented roast chicken. "We have kept everything pretty simple. I just need to order my dress."

"Isn't that supposed to be the most difficult?" Adam raised his eyebrows.

"I have been busy," Jenny said apologetically. "There's so much going on."

"Are you still playing Nancy Drew?" Adam asked irritably.

His visage had changed from romantic to grouch in a fraction of a second.

"There's very little to find," Jenny said honestly. "There are hardly any suspects and no motive. You should know. Your top suspect turned up dead."

"I was wrong about Ocean," Adam said readily. "Not entirely though. He wasn't completely blameless."

"What do you mean?"

"I told you we ran a background check, remember? His real name was Daniel Garcia. He is from California."

"I think he mentioned that once," Jenny nodded. "Not his name. Where he is from. I did think that Ocean was an assumed name."

"Daniel Garcia has a record as long as my arm," Adam said grimly. "He was involved in a lot of petty crimes. Confidence schemes, petty theft, blackmail. The police found it hard to track him because he was always on the move. Wonder how he landed in Pelican Cove."

"He may have been a crook," Jenny said. "But I believe Ocean was good at heart. He was just trying to survive."

"What are you saying, Jenny?" Adam asked angrily. "It is okay to steal if you are doing it for survival?"

"I didn't mean that," Jenny said quickly. "I mean Ocean didn't deserve to die like this."

"Don't tell me you are going to look for his killer too?" Adam said with a groan.

Jenny said nothing. She had already decided that she would try to find out what happened to Ocean.

Adam and Jenny were both quiet on the drive back. Jenny figured Adam wasn't too happy with her when he didn't stop for a walk at their favorite beach.

Jenny slept well that night and woke before her alarm went off. She reached the café on time and hummed a tune as she baked muffins for breakfast. She flung the doors open at 6 AM and greeted her first customer of the day.

"Good Morning, Captain Charlie. Here is your coffee and your chocolate chip muffin. All packed and ready to go."

"You seem chipper this morning," the old sailor said with a smile. "Counting down to the big day?"

Jenny blushed.

"I am so busy here I barely have time to think about the wedding," she confessed.

"I know what's keeping you busy," Captain Charlie said with a glint in his eye. "No luck this time, eh?"

"Are you talking about Tyler?" Jenny asked. "You are right. I am stumped. No suspects and no motive."

"What about that other fella?" Captain Charlie asked. "Heard he was done in too."

"You heard right," Jenny nodded. "Did you know

Ocean?"

"Talked to him a few times," Captain Charlie said with a nod. "He was camping out in the woods by my cabin. He had me over for a pint."

"I thought he was living out of his van," Jenny said.

"It's more like a bus," Captain Charlie explained. "What they call a camper van. He had a bed inside and everything. But this weather, he just put out a sleeping bag and slept under the stars. Said it was the best sleep a person could have."

"Did anyone else visit him while you were there?"

"I don't think so. He didn't know anyone locally. Said his friends were drifters like him, driving around the country. They met once every year, at a different location. They were meeting at Corpus Christi in November."

Jenny said goodbye to Captain Charlie and went inside. Star arrived as she began mixing batter for her blueberry pancakes. Breakfast was a blur and Jenny barely had time to gulp some coffee down.

The Magnolias arrived at 11, ready for their mid-morning break. Heather was smiling again. Betty Sue was muttering as she clacked her knitting needles.

"Her head's in the clouds," she said to Jenny. "What am I going to do with this girl?"

"Bobby Joe said Hi to me again," Heather crowed. "I think we are going to be friends."

"Why haven't we seen him around town?" Jenny asked.

"He's busy working in that bus of his all day," Betty Sue said. "Goes straight to his room when he comes into the inn."

"What about his meals?" Jenny asked. "Surely he must eat somewhere?"

"His meals are brought in by special delivery," Heather told them. "He has hired a chef in Virginia Beach. He prepares everything according to Bobby Joe's eating plan. He follows a strict diet."

Molly had come in behind the Morse women.

"He has to, I guess," she cooed. "Have you seen his abs?"

"Not really," Heather giggled.

Molly joined her.

"Do you think he will take his shirt off at the concert?"

"He won't," Star interrupted them. "That's another ten thousand bucks we can't afford."

"Are you saying he …" Jenny was speechless.

The girls dissolved into a fit of giggles again until Betty Sue rapped her hand on the table. Jenny went in to get coffee.

"When are you going to choose a wedding dress, Jenny?" Heather asked as she licked chocolate off her fingers. "Time's running out."

"How was your date with Adam last night?" Star asked, playfully poking an elbow in Jenny's side. "Is he getting impatient?"

"You know Adam," Jenny sighed. "He wants me to stop sniffing around."

"Did he tell you anything about Ocean?" Heather asked eagerly.

"Ocean was wanted in several states," Jenny told them. "He duped a lot of people, it seems."

"That bearded oaf?" Betty Sue asked. "Why am I not surprised?"

"He was like a cuddly bear," Heather said. "And he played bad music. I listened to him a couple of times, right there on the beach."

"The music must have been a disguise," Jenny said brightly. "He entered towns as a troubadour and got to know the people."

"You think he had some devious scheme in mind for our town?" Molly asked. "We are well rid of him, in that case."

"He didn't deserve to die, Molly," Jenny said. "No one does."

"You are turning into a big old softie," Heather said. "I think being a bride is doing that to you."

Someone hailed them from the beach and the ladies looked up to see Jason waving at them. He bounded up the steps and handed over the baby carrier to Jenny.

"Hello Emily," Jenny chuckled, pinching the baby's cheeks.

"We were just talking about your client," Jenny told Jason. "Do the police have any suspects?"

"I don't think they are trying hard," Jason said frankly. "They found out he had a record."

"What are your thoughts on the subject?" Jenny asked him. "What motive could anyone have for killing him?"

"Ocean's past opens up a few possibilities," Jason explained. "He must have made some enemies."

"So you think he cheated someone and this person or persons got their revenge?"

"It's an option," Jason said.

"What was he doing on the beach that night?" Jenny asked. "I thought he camped out in the woods."

"He must have gone there to meet someone," Jason replied. "That's the most obvious explanation."

"Where was this at?" Jenny asked.

"On the edge of town," Jason informed her. "On that beach next to the bridge."

Jenny uttered an exclamation.

"Near the bridge?" she asked. "Don't you remember? That's where Ocean said he found that guitar."

"You are right, Jenny," Jason said, widening his eyes. "That can't be a coincidence."

"Maybe Ocean just liked that beach," Heather said.

"I think we are missing something," Jenny said, shaking her head. "There was something about that beach. We talked about it last time."

"It's near Peter Wilson's garage," Jason reminded her.

"That's right!" Jenny exclaimed. "We keep coming back to him, don't we?"

"You really think he is involved?"

"I don't know," Jenny admitted. "You think Ocean knew he was a crook too?"

"Ex-crook, Jenny," Jason said. "Be careful of what you say about him. He's becoming a big man now. He might be our mayor soon."

"Over my dead body," Betty Sue said dramatically. "Peter Wilson is not winning this election."

"Have you seen all the yard signs, Grandma?" Heather asked. "More and more people are supporting Peter Wilson each day. I think he's going to win in a landslide. And I thought you supported him too."

"No one's actually going to vote for an outsider," Betty Sue clucked. "This is Pelican Cove, Heather. Tradition means something here."

Molly cleared her throat.

"You people haven't heard about the green tax yet, have you?"

Every pair of eyes stared back at her.

"Peter Wilson has proposed a tax for local businesses. He says they are damaging the environment with their excessive use of plastic. So he is going to make them pay a surcharge of sorts."

"That's insane," Jenny groaned. "And we don't use plastic at the Boardwalk Café."

"You use plastic somewhere," Molly reasoned. "And all your customers don't recycle."

"I don't control where a customer throws his trash," Jenny cried.

"Exactly," Molly said. "Peter says the business should take responsibility for that."

"There's no way any business will agree to this."

"The people love it," Molly told them. "They are calling it Trash Tax and they are in favor of it. Don't forget there are only a handful of businesses compared to the number of people in town."

"This is what I am talking about," Jason told Jenny. "Peter Wilson is all set to be mayor."

"That doesn't make him innocent, Jason. And being mayor won't absolve him of murder."

"It shouldn't, Jenny," Jason agreed. "But you know

what a snob Adam is. You think he will investigate such a powerful person?"

"Adam is a highly scrupulous police officer," Jenny rushed to defend him. "How dare you question his character, Jason?"

"Look, I'm sorry, okay?" Jason backtracked. "That came out wrong. I just want you to be careful."

"I'm going to find out if Peter and Ocean knew each other. We can go talk to him after that."

"I will go with you," Jason offered. "You don't need to do everything alone."

Jenny smiled.

"I don't have to. Not when I have friends like you."

"Start by telling him you support him," Heather advised. "That will make things go smoother."

"Great idea, Heather," Jenny agreed. "I don't mind stroking his ego if it helps me get to the truth."

Chapter 18

Jenny worked nonstop all day. She served her customers with a smile but she couldn't wait to get away. She finally made her way to Williams Seafood Market to get something for dinner.

Chris Williams greeted her warmly.

"Have you heard about this Trash Tax, Jenny?" he asked. "I hope you will join us in protesting it."

Jenny assured him the local business owners could count on her support.

Chris packed her usual order of sea bass and shrimp.

"You seem preoccupied," he said as he rang up her purchase.

"I was thinking about Ocean," she admitted to Chris. "Did you ever see him talking to Peter Wilson?"

"They seemed to hit it off," Chris told her. "Saw them sharing a pint a couple of times."

"Maybe I should talk to Eddie," Jenny muttered.

She went to the Rusty Anchor, trying not to feel too hopeful. Eddie Cotton greeted her enthusiastically and offered her a drink on the house. Jenny opted for a glass of wine.

"What brings you here, little lady?" Eddie asked. "And where is your posse tonight?"

"I was hoping to pick your brain," Jenny admitted.

Eddie offered to help any way he could. Jenny asked him about Ocean and Peter Wilson.

"What did those two talk about. Any idea?"

Eddie wasn't sure.

"It was some kind of business deal, I think. Something which would benefit the both of them."

Jenny felt she had established that Ocean knew Peter. She called Jason and asked him if he had time to go visit Peter Wilson. He agreed to meet her at Wilson's Auto Shop.

Peter Wilson was working on a car when they reached the garage. Dressed in grease stained overalls with sweat lining his brow, he looked like an honest, hardworking man. He smiled when he saw the baby carrier Jason was holding. He had two daughters, one of them in college.

"They grow up really fast," he said to Jason. "She'll fly the nest before you know it."

He turned toward Jenny and smiled.

"Am I in trouble? You look fierce."

"That depends," Jenny said primly. "We are here to talk about Ocean."

Peter's expression was inscrutable.

"I was sorry to hear about him. He was a good guy."

"Did you know him well?" Jenny asked.

"Not really," Peter Wilson said with a shrug.

"He was found near here," Jason said. "Near your shop, I mean."

Peter Wilson's face hardened.

"Are you accusing me of something? This here is a public beach. I don't keep track of everyone who comes or goes here."

"So you never saw Ocean walking around here?" Jenny asked.

"I didn't, believe me. I close shop at 5 PM and go home. He might have come here after that. And I'm busy during the day. I don't sit and stare at the beach all the time."

"Eddie said you were hatching some kind of scheme with him."

"He was proposing a festival for troubadours," Peter Wilson told them. "The town would take money from them. He said he could supply at least a dozen of them singers."

"I guess he wanted money for that?" Jason asked.

Peter nodded. "Like a finder's fee."

"Why would he come to you with such a scheme?" Jason wondered.

"It's all this buzz about the election," Peter smiled. "He thought I was going to be mayor."

"Judging by all accounts, you might be," Jenny conceded.

Peter looked thoughtful as he wiped a wrench.

"I don't think so. When push comes to shove, people will vote for Barb."

"That's not a very positive attitude," Jenny remarked.

"I'm just being realistic," Peter shrugged. "And it's fine. I never thought so many people would support me. They have made me a happy man."

Jenny and Jason said goodbye to Peter. Jenny invited Jason for dinner and he accepted.

"Why don't I get us some dessert?" he offered. "You go on, Jenny. We are right behind you."

Star was happy to learn they were having company. She started helping Jenny prep for dinner. Jenny made carrot and avocado puree for the baby.

Then she made a rice pilaf and a green salad to go with the fish.

"Are you ready to cross Peter off your list now?" Jason asked as they sat down for dinner.

"I'm really not sure," Jenny grumbled. "Say we cross Peter off. What does that leave us with?"

"That's no reason to suspect him," Jason reasoned.

Jenny had to agree with him.

They gorged on the ice cream Jason had brought from the local creamery. Jason and Emily left and Jenny dragged herself upstairs, ready to turn in after a long day.

The alarm woke Jenny up the next day. She showered and dressed in her favorite pair of shorts and a chambray shirt. Labor Day had come and gone but the weather was still quite hot in Pelican Cove.

Jenny was surprised to see a line outside the café at 5 AM. Groups of people loitered on the beach. Jenny went in and started the coffee. The phone rang, startling her. It was Heather.

"Are you ready for the big day?" Heather screamed in her ear.

"What's going on, Heather?" Jenny asked. "Why are there people on the beach at this hour?"

"You don't know?" Heather asked. "Don't you check your Instagram?"

"What has happened?" Jenny asked with a sigh. "Just tell me, Heather."

"Bobby Joe is making an appearance today," Heather told her. "He has decided to have breakfast at the Boardwalk Café."

"He told you that?" Jenny asked.

"He told the whole world, Jenny," Heather giggled. "He posted it on his Insta last night. People are driving overnight to catch a glimpse of him here."

"That's why there are people on the sidewalk!" Jenny said, connecting the dots.

"Forget the people," Heather said. "What are you making for breakfast?"

"Whatever's on the calendar," Jenny said. "Wait a minute … it's crab omelets today."

"Bobby Joe likes chocolate chip pancakes," Heather informed her. "With extra chocolate chips."

"Didn't you say he was on some kind of diet?" Jenny asked sarcastically.

"Today is his cheat day," Heather quipped. "And he is willing to spend it at the Boardwalk Café. Just think of all the free publicity, Jenny."

"I'm worried about all those people outside," Jenny said. "What am I going to feed them, Heather? You better come here and help."

"On my way," Heather said. "I'm not missing this for all the gold in Pelican Cove."

Rumor had it there was a lot of gold in town. It came from sunken treasure.

Jenny managed to bake a few trays of muffins before 6 AM. People rushed in as soon as she threw the doors open. She could see Captain Charlie on the sidewalk, struggling to make his way in through the crowd. She waved at him and pointed toward the deck. He got the message and went around the café to the back.

"What's all this ruckus?" Captain Charlie asked, pulling out a chair on the deck.

"Heather says that big country singer is coming here for breakfast," Jenny told him. "These are his fans, I think."

Jenny handed over a paper bag with two muffins and a cup of coffee. Captain Charlie thanked her before heading out. He turned around just as he reached the bottom step.

"Weren't you asking about that Ocean chap? I remembered something about him."

"Go on," Jenny urged.

"Saw him in a fancy car one evening," Captain Charlie said. "At least I thought that was him at the time. But what was he doing in a car like that?"

Jenny thanked him for the information and waved goodbye.

Pandemonium reigned inside the café. They had already run out of coffee and muffins. Almost everyone wanted the crab omelets. Jenny and Heather got busy beating eggs and flipping omelets. Jenny called Star and begged her to come in and help them.

Jenny had lost count of the number of omelets she made when Heather gave a cry.

"What's wrong now?" Star asked.

She had come in and taken charge of the cash register.

Heather waved her phone at them.

"It's Bobby Joe! He just started from the inn. He should be here in five minutes."

A roar went up through the café. Most of the customers had lingered over their food, refusing to give up their vantage point. People stood along the walls, sipping coffee or lemonade and waiting for their icon to come in.

Jenny peeped outside and sucked in a breath at the scene outside. She pulled Heather to her side.

"Can you believe that?"

The street was packed with people. Many of them wore T-shirts with Bobby Joe's face or name printed on them. Some people were waving flags with his picture on them. Someone began chanting Bobby Joe's name and the crowd took it up.

Heather began snapping pictures with her phone.

"This is priceless, Jenny. You can't buy this kind of publicity!"

The crowd parted and a tall, broad shouldered young man walked through, blowing kisses to the crowd. The sun glinted off his copper colored mop. A couple of burly security guys straddled him, keeping the crowd at bay.

"We love you, Bobby Joe!" a girl cried from the crowd and began pulling off her top.

Heather pulled Jenny inside.

"Better start making those pancakes."

A table had been miraculously cleared for Bobby Joe. Jenny went out to greet him and take his order.

"How are you, sugar?" he drawled. "Nice place you got here."

Jenny fought a blush. Bobby Joe was at least 10 years younger than her but she had eyes. Jenny had to admit he was one handsome hunk.

Jenny's hands shook as she arranged the crab omelet on a plate and added toast and bacon. Another plate held a stack of chocolate chip pancakes with her special chocolate and espresso sauce, topped with whipped cream.

Fans were clicking pictures with Bobby Joe when Jenny took the food outside. Heather made her pose with him and clicked several photos of Jenny and her food with Bobby Joe. Jenny knew she would post them online on the café's page.

"Delicious!" Bobby Joe exclaimed when he took a bite of the pancakes. "Best I have tasted in my life."

Some fans wanted Bobby Joe to say something.

"I am singing at the Pelican Cove Fall Festival. It's going to be lit. See you there!"

Bobby Joe surprised Jenny by cleaning his plate. He walked out with his guards, waving at the crowd.

People who had been hogging the café all morning tagged along after Bobby Joe. A fresh wave came in, thirsty and hungry after standing out in the sun.

Jenny and her friends spent the day churning out massive quantities of food. The Magnolias didn't meet that day. There was no time to relax and no place to sit. Every single chair on the deck was taken. People sat on the steps and on the beach, eating Jenny's food and giving high praise.

"We have done more business today than we did all month," Jenny told her aunt later, wiping her brow with the back of her hand.

The café stayed open longer than usual. The crowd finally thinned as people realized their star Bobby Joe wasn't making any impromptu appearances. People began driving out of town.

Jenny stood on the deck, enjoying the cool breeze rolling off the Atlantic. She was ready to drop with exhaustion. The sun was a big ball of fire, hanging low on the horizon. The sky was streaked with pink. Jenny stifled a yawn and smiled to herself. She had survived a tough day and she was proud of herself.

Something dark flew through the air and struck her ear. Jenny yelped in pain at the impact. She looked around sharply and spotted someone running away from the café.

"Hey, you!" she called out, holding a hand to her head.

She didn't have the energy to run after her assailant. He was already a speck in the distance. Jenny collapsed into a chair, wondering who was taking potshots at her.

Chapter 19

The Magnolias were looking at Jenny with concern. It was the day after Bobby Joe Tucker had graced the Boardwalk Café with his presence. Jenny was dragging her feet, still worn out from the previous day. The Magnolias were just learning about the attack on Jenny.

"Does it hurt?" Molly asked, peering at the spot above Jenny's left ear.

"It's a bit sore, that's all."

"Have you been to the doctor?" Betty Sue demanded. "Don't take this lightly, young lady."

"Relax," Jenny told them. "It was just a mud pie."

"But what if it had been something more deadly?" Heather asked.

"I think it was just a wayward tourist," Jenny told them.

She had told herself to believe that over and over.

Star wasn't taking any of it.

"I don't think so, Jenny. What if someone is trying to warn you off?"

"Someone who?"

"Someone who's not happy with your snooping, of course," Heather said. "Looks like you have ruffled some feathers."

"I don't think so," Jenny said, shaking her head in denial. "I don't have a single suspect."

"Then who's attacking you in broad daylight?" Molly asked worriedly. "Have you told Adam about this?"

Jenny hadn't but her aunt had. Adam had given her a lecture as usual and begged her to be more careful.

"He knows," Jenny said, giving Star a withering look.

"Normally I am pretty supportive of your sleuthing," Star said. "But I think you should call it quits this time. We are almost into October. It's time you started preparing for the wedding."

"Haven't we been doing that all this time?" Jenny asked, rolling her eyes.

She held up her hand as Heather and Molly both opened their mouths to object.

"I shortlisted three wedding dresses. Let's go and try them on one last time. I will make my final choice after that."

"Shall we go today?" Heather asked eagerly. "The fall festival is two days away and I am going to be busy volunteering tomorrow onwards."

"I am not missing this," Molly said. "I am going to call in sick."

"Molly, you already went in to work this morning," Heather reminded her.

"But I feel a migraine coming on," Molly said, widening her eyes. "Don't even think of going without me, Heather."

The girls squabbled over what to do. Star convinced Jenny to take half the day off.

"Don't worry about the café," Star told her. "I can handle it."

Jenny insisted on helping her aunt prep for lunch.

"Let's start in a couple of hours," she told Heather and Molly. "I will pack some sandwiches for us. We can eat in the car."

Jenny's excitement about the trip amped up as she thought about the three dresses she had narrowed down. She covered two platters of sandwiches with plastic wrap and placed them in the refrigerator. She packed some chicken salad sandwiches for their trip, along with potato chips and cookies. She added two bottles of sweet tea to the small basket.

"All set?" Star beamed at her. "Take some pictures."

"Don't worry, I am not going to order the dress without consulting you."

Star's eyes filled up. Jenny hugged her aunt tightly, swallowing the lump in her throat. Her aunt had offered her refuge when she had been alone and miserable. She would never forget what Star had done for her. She was determined to take care of her aging aunt for the rest of her life. It was the least she could do. Estranged from her own mother, Star was the only family Jenny had other than her son.

"Have fun, sweetie!" Star said, patting her on the back.

Jenny picked up the food hamper and breezed out of the kitchen, ready to hit the road with her friends. A young girl sprang up from a table when she saw Jenny. Jenny gasped at how beautiful she was with her wispy red hair and sculpted face. Jenny guessed she was barely twenty one.

"Are you Jenny King?" the girl asked. "I have been waiting for you."

Jenny looked into her deep cornflower blue eyes and smiled tentatively.

"Have we met before?"

The girl shook her head.

"My name is Rebecca Brown. I live here in Pelican Cove. I heard you were looking for information about Tyler Jones."

"I guess you can say that," Jenny said. "I was just about to leave for an appointment though. Can we talk some other time?"

The girl hesitated.

"I am not sure I will have the courage to come back," she said honestly.

Jenny made a snap decision.

"Why don't you come with me? We can talk in the car."

The girl seemed overawed when she saw Heather and Molly waiting by the car.

"I wanted to talk in private," she said.

"Don't worry," Jenny told her. "I share everything with Molly and Heather. You don't have to worry about them."

Introductions were made and the girls welcomed

Rebecca.

"The more, the merrier," Heather said in her usual friendly manner.

"So? How did you know Tyler?" Jenny asked the girl.

"Tyler and I were engaged."

The girls stared at each other with wide eyes and raised eyebrows. They hadn't expected this.

"We know Tyler was seeing someone," Jenny told her. "But we had no idea he was engaged."

Tears streamed down the girl's face.

"Tyler was such a gentleman. He proposed when we found out I was pregnant."

Jenny dropped any pretense of being cool.

"You're expecting Tyler's child?" she asked incredulously. "How does anyone not know this?"

"Who am I going to tell?" the girl asked.

"The family, of course," Jenny cried. "Old Mr. Jones will be very happy."

"Tyler's grandpa?" Rebecca asked. "We were going to meet him soon. Tyler adored him."

"I can give you his number," Jenny offered.

"Billy said I should wait."

"You know Billy?" Jenny asked.

"I have met him a few times," Rebecca told them.

She looked like she had a bad taste in her mouth. Jenny guessed their dislike for each other was mutual.

"What do you do, Rebecca?"

"I am a college student. I was home for my summer break when I met Tyler."

"What was he like?" Jenny asked.

"Very shy," Rebecca told them. "You would never have guessed he performed in front of a crowd. He was so passionate about his music."

"So you like music too?" Jenny asked.

"We had that in common," Rebecca nodded. "I am going to minor in music. Tyler and I both loved the blues. His own music was a peculiar blend of country and pop."

"You started dating, then?"

"We hit it off right away. Tyler and I used to meet on

one of the beaches after sunset."

"When did you find out about his background?"

"There were little signs," Rebecca told them. "His clothes, the really expensive watch he wore, the way he gave away most of the money he earned during the day … he would buy ice cream for the kids or give someone a ridiculous tip."

"So you realized he was rich," Jenny said frankly.

"He told me himself," Rebecca explained. "Right on our second date. He told me about some big trust money that was coming to him in a few weeks."

Was that the only reason Rebecca had fallen in love with him, Jenny asked herself cynically.

"Why did he tell you that? I guess he didn't want to come across as a poor musician."

"He wanted to make it on his own," Rebecca explained. "He told me it was really hard to do in the music industry. But he had a safety net. He didn't want me to worry about the future."

"Was Billy helping him with his music?"

"Billy?" Rebecca asked with disdain. "Billy only helps himself. He came into a big trust when he was twenty five, about five years ago. Tyler said he had squandered it all. Now he was after Tyler's money."

"So they didn't get along?" Jenny asked.

"Not really," Rebecca told her. "Tyler wanted Billy to take an interest in the family business. He felt that would allow him to focus on his music. But Billy doesn't want to work at all."

"How did Tyler get on with his uncle?" Jenny asked.

"Tyler's parents died when he was a child. His uncle was his big role model. The uncle wanted Tyler to start learning the business."

"And Tyler didn't want to?"

"He just wanted to do something on his own first. He had given himself six months. He was hoping to have a hit single in that time. He said he would happily take up the family business after that."

Jenny remembered how Tyler had been hung up on being the only troubadour in town.

"Do you know why he came to Pelican Cove?"

"Tyler discovered this town by accident when he took a wrong turn. He loved the vibe here. Said this town had become his muse."

"Was he making a lot of new music?" Jenny asked curiously.

"He recorded a song," Rebecca smiled sadly. "He was very excited about it. He was looking for a contract with some record label."

Heather had been driving the car while Jenny and Rebecca chatted in the back seat. She had reached a designer's studio two towns over. It was going to be their first stop that day.

Jenny took Rebecca by the arm and coaxed her to go in with them. The dress was tried on and pronounced beautiful. Heather took several pictures for Star.

"Are you ready to lock this one down?" Molly asked.

Jenny shook her head.

"I am going to try on all three dresses."

"Let's get going then," Heather quipped. "No time to waste."

Heather offered to drop Rebecca back in Pelican Cove before heading out to the city. Rebecca agreed gratefully.

"Where have you been hiding all this time?" Jenny asked her. "Why didn't you come forward before this?"

"Billy warned me to stay under the radar," she explained. "He said the tabloids would start harassing me."

Jenny's opinion of Billy Jones was changing rapidly.

"What made you seek me out now?" Jenny asked.

"You know how active the local grapevine is," Rebecca said. "Talk was that you were trying hard to find Tyler's killer. Everyone said you were really good at it. So I was just watching from a distance. Then someone said you have given up."

"There are no suspects," Jenny explained. "My wedding is just a few weeks away and the café keeps me busy."

"You are the only hope I have," Rebecca pleaded. "Please don't give up yet. I want to see Tyler's killer brought to justice."

"I can't promise anything, but I will see what I can do."

Jenny urged Rebecca to go meet the Jones family at the earliest. They entered Pelican Cove and dropped her off in the town square.

"What did you think of that girl?" Heather asked as they sped toward the Chesapeake Bay Bridge -Tunnel that would take them into Virginia Beach.

"She's so young," Jenny exclaimed. "She looks innocent."

"Are you going soft, Jenny?" Molly laughed. "Looks don't mean anything."

"What motive could she possibly have to harm Tyler?" Jenny asked. "She was marrying into millions. Now she is alone with a baby on the way."

"You just have her word for it," Heather argued. "What if Tyler broke up with her, huh?"

"Maybe that child isn't Tyler's at all," Molly offered. "She could have killed Tyler to get him out of the way. Now she can act the role of the poor widow and extract money from the Joneses."

"You are both crazy," Jenny dismissed.

"You taught us well, Jenny," Heather told her smugly. "Never take anyone at face value. Confirm it from different sources."

"Billy tried to paint Rebecca in a bad light. She is doing the same thing with him. Looks like they are trying to throw each other under the bus."

Heather turned toward Jenny as she pulled up in front of a toll booth.

"What if they are both lying?"

Chapter 20

The day of the fall festival arrived.

The town of Pelican Cove was packed to the gills. A sea of people thronged the town square. There wasn't a single empty spot left to stand on. The Boardwalk Café was bursting at the seams. Every table on the outdoor deck had been taken. People had set up camp chairs on the beach surrounding the deck. They bought food from the front counter and feasted on it at the beach.

Jenny was working like an automaton, helped by her aunt Star and her friends Heather and Molly. Betty Sue presided over the cash counter. Jenny had finally made several batches of truffles in honor of the occasion. Five dozen boxes had been sold out within the hour.

"We are running out of bread," Heather declared as she tore open a fresh loaf. "Only two loafs remaining."

"Those are our last ones," Jenny said. "Let's finish making these sandwiches and call it quits."

"People are still coming in," Star said, taking a peep outside.

"I can't help it," Jenny said. "We are out of everything.

Time to let our hair down and enjoy the festival ourselves."

"Have you seen that stage they erected on the beach?" Molly asked. "We have never had anything like it before."

Jenny shook her head. She hadn't even gone out on deck all day.

"Bobby Joe's people had precise instructions on how to build that stage," Heather told them. "Mandy managed all that."

"What would we do without Mandy!" Jenny exclaimed.

Star made a face. She had reluctantly delegated any work related to the concert to Mandy.

"This is going to be the best fall festival ever!" Heather crowed.

They were all beginning to get excited about the concert. Finally, the last morsel was served and the Magnolias breathed a sigh of relief. They had all brought dresses to change into for the festival. The girls primped and got ready in half an hour and set off.

The mercury had finally dipped a bit in Pelican Cove, bringing some much awaited cool weather. It was a sunny evening and the crowd was getting excited as the musicians tuned their instruments.

A roar went up in the crowd as Bobby Joe appeared on stage. He started playing his guitar and the crowd erupted in a roar.

Molly stood arm in arm with Chris. Jason wasn't coming because he hadn't found a sitter for Emily. Adam was on crowd control duty. Star and Betty Sue were going to relax on the café's deck and listen to the music from a distance.

Someone tapped Jenny on the shoulder. She turned around, hoping it was Adam. It was Barb Norton.

"Isn't this great, Jenny?" she tittered. "Don't forget who brought this famous country music star to Pelican Cove. It was all my idea."

Jenny knew that wasn't true but she went along with it.

"This concert is going to be a big boost for tourism," Barb continued. "How's the take at the café been these past two days? Better than the whole summer, huh?"

Jenny had to agree with Barb.

"When I am mayor, I will be doing plenty more activities to boost tourism in the area."

"Thanks, Barb," Jenny said. "You can count on my vote."

Barb moved on to tackle her next prospect.

Things were heating up on stage. Jenny wasn't a country music fan so Bobby Joe's music wasn't very familiar to her. But she found herself tapping her foot and enjoying the atmosphere. She realized that was the beauty of a live music show.

There was another tap on Jenny's shoulder. It turned out to be Peter Wilson.

"You see all this, Jenny?" he demanded angrily. "They are destroying our environment, trashing the beach and the natural beauty of our surroundings."

Jenny nodded meekly.

"These are the dangers of excessive tourism. This is exactly what I want to curb when I am mayor. No crazy music concerts, that's for sure."

"You are right, Peter. We don't need these crowds."

"So I can count on your vote, right?" Peter asked directly.

"Sure," Jenny said.

Peter stood with his arms folded, glaring at the people around him. A couple stopped swaying to the music and moved away.

Up on the stage, Bobby Joe tapped the microphone and cleared his throat.

"Thank you all for coming. This is the one you have all been waiting for. My latest hit single."

The cheer that went up through the crowd was deafening. Peter Wilson turned red as a tomato. Jenny watched in amazement as he curled his hands into fists and pointed them at the stage.

The music started and the crowd grew quiet as Bobby Joe began crooning. He was barely two lines into the song when Peter let out a loud groan.

"Not this again. I'm fed up of listening to this crap."

Heather turned around and glowered at Peter.

"This is 'You are my everything'. It's top of the charts. Bobby Joe might even win a Grammy for it."

"So that kid was in cahoots with this goon all along?" Peter demanded.

"What are you saying, Peter?" Jenny asked.

She had lost track of what Peter was fussing about.

"This is the same song that kid who died played all summer. It's burned into my brain. You know why? Because he stood outside my house and sang that same thing from sunrise to sunset. The same thing over and over."

"That's impossible!" Heather argued. "Bobby Joe released this song just a few days ago. Tyler couldn't have played it before that."

"What did I say?" Peter frowned. "It's burned into my brain. You want proof? Let me show you."

People around them were beginning to turn around asking them to shush. A couple of security guards surrounded them suddenly and asked them to stop causing a disturbance.

Peter looked like he was ready to burst.

"Let's go back to the café," Jenny said, grabbing his arm. "You stay here and enjoy the show," she told Heather.

Peter Wilson was already pulling a phone out of his pocket. He went into the café with Jenny and started playing a video. He thrust the phone into her face.

Tyler appeared on the screen. He was standing by the gazebo in the town square, playing his guitar. Jenny watched for a while, her eyes widening in surprise.

"This does sound like the song that country star is playing right now," she admitted grudgingly.

"What did I tell ya?" Peter crowed triumphantly.

"Do you know where Tyler heard this song?"

"He wrote it himself," Peter told her. "All his music was original. He used to boast about it."

"It's actually a great song," Jenny said. "What is it you don't like about it?"

Peter looked abashed.

"It's a good song," he said reluctantly. "Even I can see that. But you listen to anything twelve hours a day, day after day after day, it begins grating on your nerves. Know what I mean?"

"I think so," Jenny said.

She was trying to figure out how Bobby Joe had got hold of Tyler's song. Peter made it easy for her.

"So what? You think that hotshot country star stole this kid's song?"

"Sure looks like it, huh?" Jenny said. "I'm going to find Adam."

She didn't have to go too far. Adam burst into the café just then, looking for her.

"What's going on, Jenny?" he bellowed. "Heather said

it had something to do with Tyler Jones?"

Jenny quickly brought him up to speed.

"Let's wait for the show to be over," Adam told them. "I will bring him in after that."

Captain Charlie barged into the café next.

"Remember that fancy car I told you about, Jenny?" he asked urgently. "The one I saw Ocean riding in?"

Jenny nodded.

"It's parked in the town square, near that big stage."

"Let's check it out," Adam said purposefully.

He strode out and Jenny, Peter and Captain Charlie followed him. It was a red Ferrari and it had been parked close to the stage. A few questions to the crowd revealed that the car belonged to Bobby Joe Tucker.

"Are you sure this is the same car?" Adam asked Captain Charlie.

He shrugged.

"Sure looks like it. We don't have another car like this in town."

"I think you should head home now, Jenny," Adam

told her. "Things might get ugly here."

The Magnolias had already planned a spa night at Seaview, Jenny's home. They ordered pizza from Mama Rosa's and made strawberry daiquiris. Molly mixed her special face packs for all of them.

Three hours later, the ladies lay sprawled around the room, stuffed with pizza and Star's caramel pumpkin pie. Star and Betty Sue had each commandeered a couch while the younger girls lay on the plush carpet.

The doorbell rang and Adam came in, looking tired and hungry.

"Tell us what happened," Betty Sue ordered. "Did that stuffed peacock kill that poor boy?"

Adam collapsed in a chair and nodded. Jenny heated some pizza for him while he began telling his story.

"Bobby Joe came to Pelican Cove sometime in the summer."

"How do we not know that?" Heather cried.

"His tour bus broke down somewhere on the highway. He came into town one evening and heard Tyler sing in the square. He thought the song had potential."

"So what? He just stole it from Tyler?" Jenny asked, incensed.

"Not at first," Adam said. "Bobby Joe offered to buy the song from Tyler. Apparently, it's a thing. These street singers often sell their music to big stars. They don't have the money to record them or market them. And they need to survive."

"So Bobby Joe thought Tyler would sell him his music," Jenny said, catching on.

"That's right," Adam nodded. "But he didn't know Tyler's background. Tyler had more than enough money to buy his own record label. And I guess that was his long term plan."

"So Tyler refused to sell," Heather summed up. "What did Bobby Joe do?"

"He came here a few times, trying to convince Tyler," Adam explained. "They had a fight where Tyler called him names. Bobby Joe strangled him in a fit of anger. He said he just lost control."

"What about Ocean?" Jenny asked. "Did he kill him too?"

"Ocean's murder was more cold blooded," Adam told them. "He was familiar with Tyler's music. He caught on to Bobby Joe as soon as he heard his hit single. He wanted to blackmail him."

"Bobby Joe wasn't willing to pay him?" Jenny asked.

"He did steal the song."

"Bobby Joe paid him once," Adam sighed. "But Ocean got greedy. Bobby Joe agreed to pay him a big sum to make him go away. They were supposed to meet at that beach near the bridge. Bobby Joe saw an opportunity and finished him off."

"Why did Bobby Joe come back to Pelican Cove after killing Tyler?" Heather asked. "Shouldn't he have gone miles away from here?"

"We asked him that," Adam told them. "He was hoping to get inspired and write some good music here, just like Tyler did. Personally, I think he got cocky. He thought he was invincible."

"Poor Tyler," Jenny said sadly. "He didn't deserve to die."

"Thanks to you, his killer won't roam free," Adam said, his eyes full of admiration. "You did it again, Jenny."

"We need to go to Richmond tomorrow," Jenny told the girls.

Jenny wanted to meet Tyler's grandpa and explain everything. Tyler's last wish had come true in a roundabout way. His song was Number 1 on the charts. Mr. Jones would use his resources to make sure

Tyler got credit for it.

Jenny was looking forward to a pit stop on the way. She had chosen her wedding dress. She couldn't wait to order it.

Jenny gave Adam a secret smile. Their big day was just around the corner.

Epilogue

It was a mild fall day in Pelican Cove. The weatherman predicted a pleasant day with highs in the 60s. Cool winds blew in from the north, making the air a bit chilly.

A small group of people had assembled in the garden by the beach. They wore broad smiles as they waited for the ceremony. A beautiful arch decorated with roses and gardenias was erected at one end. The pale peach voile draped around the arch matched the giant bows tied to the chairs.

Jenny's son stood on one side, ready to give her away. Betty Sue had been chosen to officiate the wedding. She looked imposing as usual in a red silk dress and matching hat.

Jenny's closest friends waited inside the house with her. Adam's daughters looked beautiful in matching yellow dresses. Heather and Molly wore shades of russet and Star was dressed in a vibrant orange gown.

The bride was trying to quell the butterflies in her stomach. She was a vision in ivory, wearing the dress of her dreams. Long sleeved with a sweetheart neckline, it had a three foot long train and a bodice embroidered in tiny pearls. She wore a tiara on her head and a rose from the garden was tucked into her hair.

Everyone was eagerly waiting for the groom. His brother Ethan was going to drive him over.

An hour later, they were still waiting for Adam. Ethan Hopkins arrived with a screech of brakes. He looked at Star and shook his head.

Heather's phone rang just then. Her face turned ashen as she listened to the voice at the other end. She stared at Jenny, unable to utter a word.

"That was Adam," she finally whispered.

A single tear rolled down Jenny's face as she took in her friend's dismay.

"He's not coming, is he?"

***

Thank you for reading this book. If you enjoyed this book, please consider leaving a brief review. Even a few words or a line or two will do.

As an indie author, I rely on reviews to spread the word about my book. Your assistance will be very helpful and greatly appreciated.

I would also really appreciate it if you tell your friends and family about the book. Word of mouth is an author's best friend, and it will be of immense help to me.

Many Thanks!

Author Leena Clover

http://leenaclover.com

Leenaclover@gmail.com

http://twitter.com/leenaclover

https://www.facebook.com/leenaclovercozymysterybooks

Acknowledgements

I would like to thank my indefatigable sibling for the constant support and encouragement which went a long way toward the release of this book. Thanks to my readers for waiting patiently for this one. These are the people who motivate me day after day and inspire me to write.

Books by Leena Clover

Pelican Cove Cozy Mystery Series

Strawberries and Strangers – Pelican Cove Cozy Mystery Book 1

https://www.amazon.com/dp/B07CSW34GB/

Cupcakes and Celebrities – Pelican Cove Cozy Mystery Book 2

https://www.amazon.com/dp/B07CYX5TNR

Berries and Birthdays – Pelican Cove Cozy Mystery Book 3

https://www.amazon.com/gp/product/B07D7GG8KV

Sprinkles and Skeletons – Pelican Cove Cozy Mystery Book 4

https://www.amazon.com/dp/B07DW91NKG

Waffles and Weekends – Pelican Cove Cozy Mystery Book 6

https://www.amazon.com/dp/B07FRJ1FC1/

Parfaits and Paramours – Pelican Cove Cozy Mystery Book 7

https://www.amazon.com/dp/B07K5G2DDJ

Have you read all the Meera Patel books?

Gone with the Wings – Meera Patel Cozy Mystery Book 1

https://www.amazon.com/dp/B071WHNM6K

A Pocket Full of Pie - Meera Patel Cozy Mystery Book 2

https://www.amazon.com/dp/B072Q7B47P/

For a Few Dumplings More - Meera Patel Cozy Mystery Book 3

https://www.amazon.com/dp/B072V3T2BV

Back to the Fajitas - Meera Patel Cozy Mystery Book 4

https://www.amazon.com/dp/B0748KPTLM

Christmas with the Franks – Meera Patel Cozy Mystery Book 5

https://www.amazon.com/gp/product/B077GXR4WS/

Join my Newsletter

Get access to exclusive bonus content, sneak peeks, giveaways and much more. Also get a chance to join my exclusive ARC group, the people who get first dibs on all my new books.

Sign up at the following link and join the fun.

Click here →
http://www.subscribepage.com/leenaclovernl

I love to hear from my readers, so please feel free to connect with me at any of the following places.

Website – http://leenaclover.com

Twitter – https://twitter.com/leenaclover

Facebook – http://facebook.com/leenaclovercozymysterybooks

Email – leenaclover@gmail.com

Made in the USA
Monee, IL
03 March 2021